*God on Every Wind*

# God on Every Wind

## Farhad Sorabjee

PARTHIAN

Parthian
The Old Surgery
Napier Street
Cardigan
SA43 1ED

www.parthianbooks.com

First published in 2012
© Farhad Sorabjee 2012
All Rights Reserved

ISBN 978-1-908069-90-0

Editor: Kathryn Gray
Cover by www.theundercard.co.uk
Typeset by Elaine Sharples
Printed and bound by Gomer Press, Llandysul, Wales

Published with the financial support of the Welsh
Books Council

British Library Cataloguing in Publication Data

A cataloguing record for this book is available from
the British Library.

For my parents

# One

The rain came late to the last monsoon in the life of Philomena Avan DaCruz. In the evening angry clouds prowled the horizon over the Arabian Sea. But the next morning they were gone and the sun was back, sucking solace from ponds and watering holes, strafing the trees. The white-hot lanes of Shirley Rajan shimmered as they wound their age-old way through the little fishing village that spawned the beast.

It was a happy beginning, all those years ago. Fresh, and as yet untainted by greed or pride or fury or winter hearts. Long before the great trade routes were stalked, and very long before the possession of distant peoples was exchanged as gifts at imperial weddings in Europe, the little village, fanned by the swishing palms, sat contentedly on a knoll, watching over the sea.

Then came the great waves of Christian conversions that swept away Ganesh Mina and created Timotio

DaCruz, and, after him, his son Genaro, who prospered and built the great mansion on the Shirley Rajan hill which he christened the Casa de Familia DaCruz. And still nothing changed very much. The catch was good, the waters kind.

But man has no heart for resting content. Someone went north to see the great *darbars* of India. Someone stole away from the abuse of a father. Someone saw a talent in his fingers that demanded ambition of him. For such simple reasons are villages lost and kingdoms won, for their receding footprints carried the seeds that would one day whip and swirl on the winds back to Shirley Rajan to settle and suck and leave only a husk.

For the wanderers carried with them the part of man which longs for home. They spoke of it in drunken monotones in rusty inns and sour-faced tenements and tangled bazaars. A simple etching grew into a masterpiece, swept by wild and splendorous and false colours that absence had inserted into their memory: the beauty of the bay drew a million strange and unknown fish. The melody of its musicians made the palm fronds clap in joyous applause. Wrecks of great ships carrying boundless treasures lolled about in the great depths of the bay, their jewels glinting off setting suns and casting a rich glow over the air. And so a great murmur rose across the land, and carried on the winds, gathered in a mighty force on the hills outside the village.

Which is not to say that the city grew around the little village. In fact the 'good bay' from which the city took its name was probably not the Shirley Bay at all but it does not matter; such fine distinctions matter little to

2

the rampaging architects of progress. When its great leap upward commenced in the 1950s and Bombay gouged its way through salt pans and sailing masts and homesteads and habits, it skidded to a halt at the edge of Shirley Rajan, perplexed.

Quite inexplicably, Augustino 'Captain' Colaco did not see the advantages of a spanking new concrete box from where he could continue to sell his 'Home-tapped Toddy'. Taufiq Mian, village boss and revered Shirley Rajah, would not permit the old cross (INRI 1941) in the clearing at the top of the road by the sea to be demolished for a new bus stop. 'Anyway,' he said, 'we all know that old Parkar's almost blind and would run the bus into it. He only survives because we have left everything in the places his memories can see.' And when Jojo Jacinto the carpenter solemnly unsheathed the ancestral meat cleaver and purposefully sharpened it for two days and a night on the outer wall of the village, Bombay's crisp and financial agents sulkily withdrew their attentions.

Then back they came, armed with reasons. Not very good ones, but devious enough to ravish the honest order of simple minds. 'Captain' Colaco moved south, where he saw the wisdom of Bombay in the cash till of his liquor bar on the corner of sleepless Falkland Road. Taufiq Mian's organisational skills became T. G. Hafeez, Chief Foreman, Tick Tock Constructions (Pvt.) Ltd., where he operated with a ruthlessness born of hidden grief and the bitterness of bloodless surrenders. Old Parkar was retired to a home in Vasai where an unseen shelf caught an unwanted head and the memories

3

merged with his dark eyes forever. And Moin Cardozo jumped off Santan Rodrigues's fishing boat into a dawning Arabian Sea, roaring visions of Portugal.

The village slowly shrank and curled up into itself. And at the heart of its catatonic shape, the Casa de Familia DaCruz. And Philomena.

Now Philomena's own residence at the Casa de Familia DaCruz had been limited – the first part of her life and the last – and anyway most of these events had preceded her. Nor did she quite know why Tick Tock Constructions never turned its greasy attention upon the sprawling Casa de Familia DaCruz in all its many empty years between the death of her mother and her own return. Dark tales of demons and ghosts trickled about the village, but for her it had only sighed with contentment.

In the darkening hall she sat, with the faded tapestries and the chalky smell of whitewashed silences. As always, she sat by the small window that opened onto the veranda. She faced the murmuring television, mercurial flashes on her face as she watched, as ever, the news.

A spear of blue fog fell from the grime-lit glass tile in the roof, dropping a dreary, still light on a mantelpiece which derived its substance from the objects upon it.

A small box with a photograph in a tarnished metal frame, a couple of letters, a newspaper clipping, a broken silver necklace with a silver pendant in the shape of a fishing *dhow*, a note pad with some dates written on it. These were objects that only Philomena could touch and only she was allowed to dust. They waited only for her, specially possessed.

Some mornings when Kanta arrived earlier than usual to swab the floors she would watch quietly as Philomena dragged herself to the mantelpiece, a broken soldier to a remembrance ceremony. She would watch as Philomena caressed the box or read from the envelopes and see the knots move on Philomena's face as victories and regrets and whole lives dropped from every quiver of her cheek and every bite of her lip.

Behind these special things, other lives. The rusted photographs of unknown ancestors, with unknown quirks and untold stories of unimportant weaknesses. A scratch across the paper, a crack along a frame, with their own crumbling lives and twisting tales to tell.

So many stories and so many lives on a quiet mantelpiece in a cool, forgotten room in a huge, forgetting city with so many people, with so little belief in the reading of mantelpieces. Or the embers in the eyes of a fisherman's corpse.

# Two

Now of this business of life Philomena knew a thing or two. Her initial introduction to it was under the great banyan tree that sits by the side of the pebbled driveway of the Lady of Succour Nursing Home, a tree that bears the legend 'Bombay Best Tree, 1943, 1944, 1946' and carries on its gnarled shoulders the presidency of the woods that cocoon the Lady of Succour from the fretting and fuming that scours the road outside its gates.

One gentle November evening in 1942, two years before the arrival of Philomena, Edson DaCruz sat in his lolling-chair on the veranda of the Casa de Familia DaCruz, as always meticulously de-fizzing the soda in his rum with the little finger of his right hand as he drank. A clock ticked in the hall. Vessels clicked in the kitchen. On the radio, the BBC began its timeless World News tune that had conquered distant peoples in a way Empire never would. Upstairs, the maids cracked bedsheets into shape. Domesticity hung fatly in the air.

Edson gazed out over the driveway and past the gate, where the road curved and ran away down to the sea. Moin, the fisherman who sometimes helped about the house, was sitting outside his hut mending a net by the light of a burning torch. But Edson was preoccupied, and he saw neither Moin nor absorbed the detail.

He glanced nervously at his engorged wife as she knitted. 'Shouldn't you now go to the nursing home till he is born?'

Tehmina looked up and sighed. 'I'm not due for another month, and it's not a he.'

Edson started slightly, like a chess player faced with an unusual move.

'Yes, yes, all right, not a he. But there is no point in taking chances.'

Despite Tehmina's sustained derision and Dr Bendre's reassurance that no chances were really being taken yet, Edson refused to be deflected. He pursued the matter quietly, with no commands to provoke instant refusal or rages to bolster silent resolve.

In fact, Edson had never raged or commandeered in his life. He was a man with a cringing fear of unpleasantness, a man who believed in discovering others' viewpoints before expressing his own. He was, for all practical purposes and to all the world, a gentleman. Tehmina was aware of all these qualities in her husband. She knew how and when to use them as sources of strength, and when to discard them as infuriating weakness. She knew, as one person of a couple must, when the other should be indulged, when firmly overridden. She was, for all practical purposes and for all the world, the boss.

It had been these very qualities in Edson that had drawn her to him in those first few months of her job as apprentice manager at the Reay Road timber yards of Timotio & Son, Purveyors of Fine Timber, Edson's premature inheritance.

After his father Genaro had been killed by an eccentric log of superior Brazilian Purple, Edson's mother had retreated to her village in Goa, where she acquired a faithful following for her reading of oracles in the dust deposits on the doorstep of the local chapel. Her fame was not restricted in its reach, and her edicts were even carried to Bombay by the believers. 'Attention!' thundered the noticeboard in the St John churchyard from time to time. 'The faithful must gather for a rosary on so-and-so day, so-and-so March at so-and-so time. This message has been received from SOCORINHA DaCRUZ of Arpora, Betim.' No further explanations were offered or required.

Alone and rudderless, Edson wandered about the timber yards in a daze, operating with adequate but unenthusiastic efficiency until one day he noticed properly his new apprentice manager, who had long cherished this shy, wistful boss of hers. One thing led, as they say, to the romantic other, and before very long Edson was gracing Tehmina's little household far more than her mother thought appropriate. The man was not a Parsi, she grumbled. But he was always humming some fancy western tune, Beethoven or Mozart. This was a troubling negation of Goolbai's firm conviction that only Parsis appreciated western music and treated their women with respect. But this *parjat* seemed to do both! The problem was immutable – she couldn't talk to her husband Coover, who was, in her considered opinion, a cretin whose only interests were his burgeoning arthritis and the death-defying tedium of his bookkeeping job at Pirojsha Oils & Soaps.

So when Edson proposed formally one evening, Goolbai sighed with relief at the resolution of her dilemma. Edson promptly became a cultured, sophisticated gentleman and a most suitable match for Tehmina. But Cooverji, hitherto an irrelevance, let out an almighty shriek and leapt out of his chair, tottering towards Edson with deadly intent. Halfway across the room he suddenly realised that his knees should not logically be able to withstand this performance, and they faithfully responded with monumental intensity. Cooverji fell to the floor and expired a short while later of anxiety. As far as Goolbai was concerned, another problem had miraculously been nipped in the bud. Edson and Tehmina had hurriedly exchanged engagement rings on the way to feed Cooverji to the vultures at the Towers of Silence.

*

Seeing that Edson's anxiety over the delivery wasn't that important, Tehmina had initially remained tolerant towards his entreaties. 'Wouldn't it be better if she sat with her legs like this in case there was a emergency?'

9

'No, that leg-position got me this way in the first place.'
'Shouldn't there be a set of forceps in the house, just in case?' 'Good idea, till the delivery we can use them to turn coals in the kitchen.' But on and on it went, and Tehmina moved from amusement to irritation to niggling doubt and, finally, to resignation.

A full twenty days before the appointed date, Edson's maroon Morris Eight darted through the gates of the Lady of Succour Nursing Home, hiccuped violently over the water drain at the beginning of the driveway, and proceeded altogether more sedately up to the entrance. Tehmina was fussed and cooed into the delivery ward by Sister Grace, Sister Mercy and Sister Pi ty (the missing 'e' having expressed its own opinion by dropping off in disgust during one of the good nurse's frequent exertions with sundry ward boys in the storeroom). Tehmina was peppered with a barrage of wholly irrelevant questions.

'When did the contractions start, dear?' Sister Grace opened.

'Any earlier false alarms? What do you feel?' Sister Mercy countered.

'Any history of high blood pressure?' Sister Pi ty with the overcall.

'Call Dr Bendre,' said Sister Grace, closing the bidding.

Tehmina held up a weak hand. 'It isn't necessary,' she said. 'I'm three weeks shy.'

'Fine,' said Sisters Mercy and Pi ty, reaching for their record sheets.

'Oh, for heaven's sake!' said Sister Grace, slapping her forehead. 'Shift her to the general ward for now – there is no place in Delivery for this sort of nonsense!'

All three drifted out of the room, bringing into view Edson, who had been watching the proceedings with critical interest.

'Never mind them,' he said, patting Tehmina's shoulder. 'They don't understand the correct approach to this sort of thing.'

In Room No. 8 of the general ward ('Deluxe Room – twin sharing basis'), Tehmina lay in wait for her baby. Every evening, after the last drunken flap of the late bird in the Gulmohur tree outside her window, Edson would arrive. She learned how to make her eyes project the correct mixture of affection and enfeeblement when she smiled back at his trifling concerns. She nursed and soothed his fears and anxieties. She murmured to him late into the night until he was drowsy enough to not resist her suggestion that he go home. When he left she lay awake composing falsehoods about the hectic nocturnal activities of the baby to recount to Edson on his morning visit. She wondered whether all men became babbling wrecks in the face of impending fatherhood. It was obviously another of God's misguided attempts to balance the books: the females will bear the burden of the birth and the males will worry to death, or the female form will have the aesthetic appeal and the male can have the raging libido as compensation. Well, she thought, that's what comes from trying to provide neat theoretical solutions without having any practical experience.

Tired of entertaining herself with such idle thoughts and staring through the window and the trees outside, Tehmina would turn over and face her roommate, and it was through her conversations with him that she discovered the horrible secret of hospitals.

Mr Muncherji Titina had entered the place with what appeared to be nothing more life-threatening than a particularly severe case of flatulence (brought on, according to him, by 'hitting up his fifty'). He was examined by the doctor who immediately ordered thirteen different tests. During test numbers four, eight and eleven, a second doctor (supervising) decided that a further six tests would be absolutely essential.

After hearing this instalment of the Titina Saga, Tehmina suggested to Edson that it would perhaps be better if she went home and came back later.

Three days after the tests, a third doctor prescribed to a much-perforated Muncherji four different medical preparations. And a further two tests. Muncherji recounted how a martyred thrill had run down his spine at the time, to be replaced by alarm after a cursory comparison of the prescription and the labels on the resultant medicines.

That evening Tehmina eyed her own meagre array of medicine suspiciously and told Edson that she was perfectly well and would not be taking take her usual evening dose.

Muncherji had shown excellent progress. The unbridled fury of the explosions from within had subsided, to the overwhelming relief of his haggard roommate. The doctors seemed to be indifferent to Muncherji's recovery. Then Muncherji developed incontinence, and their eyes glinted again.

Tehmina bribed Sister Pi ty with her mother-of-pearl comb to let her look at her prescription. Her darkest fears were confirmed – the labels on the bottles bore no resemblance whatsoever to what was on the prescription. On reflection, nothing she had ever seen bore the slightest resemblance to what was on the prescription. She realised with horror that the thing was custom-designed to give full rein to the creative and interpretative powers of the compounder. She could, for all anyone knew, be being treated for stomach distention. She felt her heart and her bowels begin to switch places, the process reaching its messy conclusion just as Edson arrived for his evening coo.

Tehmina mastered the art of talking to Edson while holding assorted mixtures in her mouth. She cultivated the habit (admired by Edson) of avoiding drinking any water to wash down the medicine. She developed the habit (adored by Edson) of rinsing out her mouth immediately after taking her medicine.

His hypochondria fortified by the bona fides of the allergic reaction, Muncherji had contracted his first real infection – he began to actually enjoy being ill. It soothed his fevered brow. It made him feel whole again. His admiration for his doctors knew no bounds. He savoured each new drug, rolling it expertly around the ever-expanding section of his tongue that housed his medicinal taste buds. He could effortlessly pronounce on the vintage of the base powder in the mixtures. He analysed bouquets and identified which compounder's vat it came from. He moaned with pleasure at the full-bodied, nutty ripeness of a confection from the Gonsalves Valley. He had near-spiritual experiences with the special smoky peatiness of what he pronounced was 'quite definitely a Highland confection' (he was right – Binay Pershad, its creator, was from Nepal). And so it went, on and on. His illnesses showed remarkable progress. At the last count he had toxicity caused by constipation, an enlarged liver caused by the alcohol in his medicine, nascent arthritis and gout caused by his ancestry, and chronic inflammation of the respiratory tract caused by his penchant for bouquets. But his heart was singing. 'Nothing wrong here, huh, nothing wrong here!' he told Tehmina, vigorously fisting his chest.

Tehmina was appalled. She would twist away from the drugged happiness on Muncherji's gnomic face in the middle of his monologues and stare at the same leaves on the tree outside. She would whirl around again and be faced again with Muncherji's medical madness. Above her head and beyond her feet, sheer unforgiving walls bore in upon her with evil intent. She would escape to the corridors outside, only to catch glimpses of more carnage through flashing doors. Tubes slickly slipped up nostrils flared with pain. Rough swabs of spirit preparing weak flesh for purges. Sly knife nicks bringing colour to blanched, grey skins. Everything so purposeful, so practised, so... clinical. Every instruction and command whispered, like in some sinister laboratory with a dark hidden agenda – an agenda she had stumbled upon through Muncherji's tale.

She spent hours in the bathroom, her cheek pressed against the right edge of the window from where she could watch the goings-on at the bicycle stand in the compound. She begged Edson for fresh air, and he walked her through the corridors of fear outside her room. She began to sense when the germ of a visit to her was sprouting in the mind of a doctor many corridors away, and the bile would instantly begin to rise with her heartbeat. She willed her baby out of her, but her body resisted her mind.

Late one December night, watching another dose of medicine swirl down the drain in the bathroom basin, Tehmina crumpled to the floor and turned to Edson for strength for the first time in her life. Broken and wracked by fear and exhaustion, and in a place where niceties like dignity no longer mattered, she howled and screamed for him to just take her home. Edson saw this as the irrationality that he had heard often overcame expectant mothers.

He called for a doctor.

Something snapped somewhere. Convulsion after convulsion slammed through Tehmina's body, and in her darkest moment of abject terror, her torn and tormented body delivered up its burden.

The doctor arrived, offering comfort and wielding a scalpel. Tehmina pushed herself back against the bathroom wall, the baby jerking along with her. The doctor stepped forward and severed the cord, leaving the baby lying in its grime amongst the purple flowers on the white tiles. Edson darted forward, whinnying. Tehmina looked at her baby. It was slimy. And it was a 'he'.

# Three

Perhaps he had absorbed the vapours around him during his mother's long internment, or perhaps Tehmina's frantic phobias had run into his veins, but Lancelot Newton DaCruz, apple of the eye of Edson, lord-in-waiting of the Casa de Familia DaCruz, was a sickly child. No one understood why he cried when bounced except Tehmina, who quite logically (and correctly) presumed that it hurt him. At three months he was little heavier than when he was born. After the sixth month, he put on a spurt that rekindled Edson's fading belief that he would be a sportsman one day. At nine months he developed whooping cough. On his first birthday Edson bought him a bright orange football, which he proceeded to ignore despite Edson's attempts to excite him with its ability to do such wondrous things as roll and bounce. He was a listless child, only willing to crawl to the bedside table and fiddle for hours with what seemed to be his only points of interest – gripe water bottles and liniment jars.

The apple of Edson's eye slowly soured. Indifference crept into Edson's attitude. His sessions with Lancelot extolling the greatness of Mathews and Mannion became less frequent, his attitude more peevish. Long after Tehmina had retired to her bed, Edson would shut himself away with his gramophone, and Elgar and Tchaikovsky would rise through the crackles and pops, and float over the British-Portuguese-Indian night. His bridge sessions at the gymkhana became longer. Fuelled by the twists and turns of the war and its arrival in Burma, his evenings with Withnall, a senior engineer with the railway, became rambling, timeless affairs. On Sundays he drove his family to church. On Friday evenings he drove his family to the golf links. On random occasions he drove his family to the doctor. Dinners became silent, clinky affairs with muttered segues of today's tedium and tomorrow's intentions.

*

Provoked by the vacuum of their lives, Tehmina reached a decision – she would seduce Edson.

She reached deep into her memory to execute the decision. Edson had liked her to be aggressive and obvious – like all gentle men, seeing the abandonment of a lover was an achievement in itself.

As the details came back to her, she stole out to the garden swing at the far end of the garden. There, swinging gently to avoid the thorns of the bougainvillea behind her catching on her clothes, she wrote:

1.   likes his ears licked
2.   likes seeing my breasts exposed – dinner ??
3.   likes me to be on top
4.   doesn't like his _____ licked
5.   doesn't like lingering before
6.   likes me to want him to slap my behind during
7.   likes me to be vocal during
8.   likes to smoke immediately after
9.   prefers that I have an orgasm
10.  doesn't like to have to go on after his

She memorised the list, then burned it during a quiet moment in the kitchen.

On the appointed evening, Tehmina wore an old russet dress whose neckline dropped too far and sagged when she leaned over. She had carefully weakened the top buttons till they hung by threads. She sat on an old cane reclining chair, feet cocked upon the wrought-iron railing of the veranda. The lamp in the porch cast a lazy amber light over her. She sipped her third sherry (remembering that liquor always assisted items 3, 6 and 7 on the list) and waited for Edson to arrive.

The sultry October stillness glistened off her neck and torso. She was careful not to disturb it – she knew that the sight had the power to cause less ponderous men than Edson to break instantly.

'Hello dear,' said Edson as he ascended the stairs.

His eyes flickered when he looked at her. A feather had been ruffled.

Gooood, thought Tehmina, leaning forward to massage an imaginary mosquito bite on the bulge of her calf.

'Lancelot asleep?' asked Edson, returning to the veranda with a drink.

'Mmm,' said Tehmina, throwing her head back and gazing at the Mangalore-tiled roof above her. She casually rearranged her legs so her dress flapped open over a thigh.

Edson wiped his brow and called for dinner.

At the best of times the old ceiling fans in the dining hall with the upturned ends radiated more majesty than air. That night, toiling over a cauldron of food and calculated seduction, they merely swirled the steamy concoction around the room.

When dessert was served, Tehmina dismissed the servants for the night. Edson looked down to his plate to spoon up the juices and Tehmina snapped the weakened buttons on her dress. Leaning forward, she spilt her breasts onto the table. Her eyes ripped into Edson and flashed through to his groin. A drop of sweat gathered body and rolled by a nipple.

She rose as Edson rose, and long-buried memories resurfaced for a moment. Then the items on the garden-swing list took over. The 'dos' were done and the 'don'ts' were avoided. Preliminaries were abandoned and positions taken. Unpleasant areas avoided and sensitive areas reviewed. Formalities observed and requirements fulfilled. The rules of engagement observed and the ceasefire respected. It was spontaneous explosion of pre-arranged carnality. Only once was Tehmina unfaithful to the script, when she became caught up in the drenched tangle of hair and skin and muscle and cried out in truth. Then it was all back on track.

19

Later Tehmina lay awake in bed, feeling empty. Smiling bitterly into the darkness, she fell asleep with her deceptions.

A new awkwardness developed between the two, and the discovery that Tehmina was pregnant again did nothing to lift the spell. Broken by his disappointments with Lancelot Newton DaCruz, Edson remained withdrawn and indifferent to the prospect of another child. He quietly agonised about their moment of abandonment and worried about a child conceived of such a passion. Tehmina, for her part, was haunted by the coldness of her designs and the prospect of another internment in hospital. A gaunt and colourless fist enveloped the Casa de Familia DaCruz.

*

Edson never spoke of that night again, and Tehmina was grateful for that. She did all that was required of her, joining Edson in social engagements, feeding Lancelot, running the household. All the time, she was aware of the growing presence of the child inside her. When it became difficult for her to follow Lancelot's expeditions to far corners of the Casa de Familia DaCruz, Edson suggested that they hire a nanny. So it was that Hilla came to the DaCruz household, and suddenly Tehmina had nothing to do.

Hilla's magical presence was a magnet to Lancelot. Age had drawn lines of tender dignity on her face, lines given only to very special people. Lancelot abandoned Tehmina completely, as though she had only been a stopgap arrangement before the real love arrived. Hilla could thrill him with a look. Control him with a whisper. She was reliable and honest. She cooked and supervised and hectored and cajoled feats of domestic brilliance out of the servants, and they loved her. She sat and talked long evenings with Tehmina about the people in the village and who had bought whose used bicycle and the wisdom of the deal, and Tehmina loved her. She found herself talking endlessly to Hilla, and more than once had to stop herself from revealing things best kept to herself. Hilla would shuffle in at Edson's calling and effortlessly locate misplaced records and books for him, and he too loved her.

Hilla steadily took over the Casa de Familia DaCruz. Tehmina no longer bothered herself with the running of the house, and Hilla became the member-in-charge of the DaCruz family. Sometimes she would go with Tehmina to the fire temple on Hill Road. This was an added advantage, for Hilla was also a Parsi and could enter the temple while Edson could not.

At the little plywood kiosk outside the temple, Hilla would gently chide Meherji the sandalwood seller about his prices. Purchases made, they would mount the marbled steps, briefly bending over and touching them in obeisance on the way in.

Entering the dark, cool rooms they would settle onto the glowing benches that flickered orange from the flames and spitting cinders of the sacred fire that the priests did not allow to ever die. They would sit a long time, praying softly in the warm glow, the scent of sandalwood and myrrh creeping into their sarees and hair. Sometimes the sound of a single gong would roll out of some deep recess of the temple signalling the beginning of a new phase of the sun, and priests in starched white muslin cassocks would rustle in. Standing before the giant silver cauldron of fire, their baritone voices would rise and roll around the sparse walls, this word clashing with the echoes of the last.

They would watch the priests' flushed pink cheeks and blazing eyes, marvel at the muslin mouth-drapes quivering with the power of the words issuing from underneath. They watched their magnificent silver beards rise and settle on the starched white cassocks. When the priests paused to gather breath or feed the fire, they would lean back and sigh into the receding echoes. As the cassocks rustled quietly, the ladies would smile to themselves, knowing that such sublime serenity could never be false in its promise of a greater world.

*

The visits to the fire temple grew more infrequent as Philomena grew inside Tehmina. She would lock herself away for hours in her room. When Hilla knocked on the door with tea, she would respond in a tone that Hilla found uneven and tremulous. When she did appear, she seemed drawn and pale. Her eyes were blank and bland, as if she had meticulously cleared them of the torment that so obviously hung about the air around her. Edson saw nothing more than the anxieties of a pregnant woman with a difficult earlier experience. Hilla, as women do, looked further and was worried.

One afternoon, Hilla crept up to Tehmina's door and pressed her ear to it. Silence reigned. Then a muffled cry. Then silence again. Hiccups. Silence. A bed thumped. Silence. The conclusive creak of the bed as someone left it. Slippers shuffled. Away. A moan cut off by a bathroom door slamming. Silence. Hilla turned away from the door as Tehmina turned to the bathroom mirror.

Not long now, she told her ravaged reflection. Her eyes dropped to the bulge of her belly. 'For you, these last days I have borne everything,' she whispered to her stomach. 'A hospital ceiling will not be your first look at life, this I promise you. And I will not suffer those days again. I will not take powders to my mouth wondering which one will kill me, or you, or both of us. I will not allow your happiness to be hunted down by my manias, like Lancelot's has. You will make us whole again.' Then the pain returned. She stuffed a towel between her teeth and cried and hiccuped into it. When the spasm passed, she straightened her hair, cleared her eyes, and went out to tea.

The days and nights dragged by. She fed her determination with her body. The lines drew longer and stronger on her face. Strange rips and holes dotted her linen and towels. Sometimes when a spasm came to her in public her eyes would roll upwards and she would quickly close them to shut away the hurt from the world.

Hilla had not missed these little signs. She considered speaking to Edson about her fears, but this would have transcended the bounds of her role, if only by a whisker.

On a dark, stormy night in the eighth month of Tehmina's pregnancy, Edson sat watching the rivers gush across the driveway and wondered when to broach the topic of Tehmina's internment. It would have to be soon. He had noticed how out of sorts she had been recently. He gazed out over the bay to the lonely flash of Danda lighthouse, besieged by the lightning-stung sea. Steady parallel streams of water poured off the tiled roof past his window and splattered fatly into the pools they had sculpted in the earth. A fine spray occasionally drifted in through the window, golden clouds in the warm light of the room. The gramophone poured out the aching adagio of Brahms' double concerto.

Into this golden sanctuary crept a strange, urgent sound. Edson started as a wail of searing intensity gathered body and rubbished Mr Brahms' feeble efforts. He jumped up and followed the sound to its source.

The howl had started in Tehmina's exhausted, fitful sleep. Awakened by it, she realised that it would have been heard anyway and let go completely. Weeks of stifled cries and swallowed pain tumbled out all together in one single sound such as none who heard it had heard before.

*

Dawn dragged a weak grey light across the twin hills of Bandra as the sweepers cleared the soggy remains of yesterday off the pavements. Edson's motor once again flew through the gates of the nursing home, this time ignoring the water-drain hiccup altogether.

Edson jumped out at the entrance and charged in to make the arrangements, leaving Hilla to watch over Tehmina who was by now a crumpled moaning heap.

All at once Tehmina felt a wetness on her thighs that she knew so well. 'It's coming!' she gasped.

Hilla's anxiety resolved itself. She gently lay Tehmina down on the wrought-iron garden bench by the driveway, and on a misty, drizzly July morning Hilla coaxed and pried Philomena from Tehmina's womb many weeks before she was due.

Tehmina was calm. Her long days and nights of suffering had been rewarded. She had not been incarcerated again in this place of purple tiles and hectic needles. No sterile walls had greeted Philomena's eyes. Her first view of the world had been of the banyan leaves above her, moist and fresh in the morning light.

The doctor arrived to sort out the details. Hilla noticed with quiet relief that the child was very fair. She had piercing grey eyes that gazed, unflinching, at the leaves above her.

The doctor finished his examination. 'Excellent!' he proclaimed, in the chunky tone that experts use when advising innocents. 'I have never seen a healthier premature baby. She is bigger than most full-term children!'

Then he bent over Philomena and wiggled a finger over her face.

'But...' he said, frowning and continuing the strange finger ritual for a long while. Finally his hand dropped to his side. He drew himself up and turned to Edson.

'The child is blind,' he said.

# Four

Edson, it must be said, was not the kind of man to hold his child's infirmity against her. He was calm and collected most times, and if he suffered now, the outer shell showed no sign of it. Tehmina too was calm, in a resigned sort of way. But it was Hilla, with her great capacity for giving without thought of return, who rose to brush off the setback. It had been her hands that were the first to hold Philomena, be anointed by her juices. In the days that followed they became the first to change her, to wash her, to feed her and burp her, and the first to wipe away the tears from her beautiful and useless eyes before smudging the tear in her own. It was Hilla who taught Philomena to sense presences. Or, more accurately, absences; for she would cry unerringly when Hilla was not there. So she didn't have to cry very much: the only significant time Hilla spent away from Philomena was at night, but then there was

Tehimina beside her, and for the night that seemed sufficient.

Hilla would lie awake long hours at night, wondering if Philomena was all right. When it became too much, she would rise and go through the slumbering rooms to Tehmina's room. Peering in through the slats of the window that opened onto the veranda she could see the crumpled moonlit figures on the beds, still and unmoving. Was she breathing? She strained to see the rise and fall of the covers, but could not. Back in her room she would toss about in her bed, aching for the morning's resolution.

Around this time began endless visits to doctors of varying expertise and strange persuasions. It was pronounced by a comforting majority that the situation was not completely hopeless: the child could quite obviously distinguish between darkness and light, though actual vision stayed stubbornly out of reach. Through all the tests and prodding and poking Philomena maintained a quiet fortitude, punctuated by the occasional bicycle kick or sigh. Finally it was decided that a second opinion should be sought in England, but after days of debate the house voted to postpone the voyage till the child was a bit older.

But much more important, Philomena was becoming a master of presences. A hunter of the airwaves. While Lancelot dully beat spoons on enamel plates, Philomena would sit motionless, her great grey eyes transfixed upon the thin air, prowling the waves. She learned to sense the nature of silences – this one placid, that one piteous, yet another tense and brooding. Densities were placed,

27

breezes read. A breath of staleness, a current of warmth. The air around her father was a network of currents: displaced musical notes wafting across a stern, even grid, soft glows washed by cool, distant winds. The space around her mother's bore a strange cross – heavy but not subsuming, sometimes punctuated with bright flames that had lost their teeth to yesterday's icy winds. And always the sound of the sea and the smell of crochet thread and bath soap. But the one she loved best was Hilla, for with her she could bask in the simple winds of love. No analysis required, no resistance called for, for no one needs resist a love that does not hedge the giving of it. Now Lancelot was a different matter. The air seemed dense and pointless, a mass whose only purpose seemed to be the occupation of space. Submerged in drudgery, colourless, vapid. An existence, not a life. Then there was Gracie the maid, and Parvati the sweeper-swabber, and Sawant the gardener, and Moin, and Santan, and Moin again...

# *Five*

At 3.03 p.m. in the turgid heat of an August afternoon in 1946, a baby boy was born in a small village somewhere in the west of Africa.

His father sat motionless by his wife, ignoring the cries of his child. The birth brought no release to the tense furrows that creased his forehead.

At 3.56 p.m. the boy's mother died.

Only then did his father turned away from her to look at his child. He gently picked up the baby and held it close. 'For a little while we were a family,' he whispered in the baby's ear.

*

A rough wind blew the sounds of celebration across the dark savannah as, clutched tight to his father's chest, a baby attended the first funeral of his life.

# *Six*

As Philomena grew more dextrous, the urge to put a shape to things grew. She would totter across to the sound of Lancelot's spoon-and-plate efforts and grab. She was already strong-willed enough to vanquish him in battles and Lancelot would relinquish his things without demur. Then Philomena would begin her exploration. First the shape of the plate, then whether it could be banged to reproduce the Lancelot sound. Disappointed with the results, she would slap the ground around her, looking for assistance. Accidentally locating the spoon on the floor, she would thump the ground with it, listening carefully for the elusive sound. Quite by chance, it would strike the abandoned plate. A smile would broaden across her face as she looked up in the direction of the applause.

The garden of the Casa de Família DaCruz proved to be a treasure trove of shapes. Wonderful smells from soft blobs attached to sticks that sometimes pricked her probing hands. The spongy floor that felt like her bed and smelled much better. But most of all she loved the moist earth from the flower beds. She would scoop up fistfuls of this rich concoction, knead it, raise fistfuls to her nose and breathe deep, then fling it upwards over herself, squealing with delight.

For two years Parvati had watched this child. Squatting on her haunches, sweeping and swabbing the vast tracts of floor at the Casa de Familia DaCruz, she would often stop and watch Philomena's acts of discovery. When she broke for her mid-morning glass of tea (half a glass, by Hilla's decree, and only one spoon of sugar), she would pad over to where Philomena was and gaze at her, sipping thoughtfully. When she spoke to Philomena it was in the matter-of-fact tone of one adult to another: in Parvati's world a child Philomena's age had already understood and accepted the rigours of its future.

Now this child, thought Parvati one day while crushing a pilfered *elaichi* into her bubbling tea, was by God's will born blind. The logical thing to do was to see if God had changed her mind (God had quite definitely to be a woman: in Parvati's experience, no man could stay sober for the length of time it must have taken to create the world).

Having decided to test the current inclination of the Almighty, Parvati had made careful enquiries. The operation commenced when, walking through the garden on her way home from work one day, she came upon Philomena playing with Lancelot's penis.

31

Walking around trouserless, Lancelot found himself with an innocent child-erection, which he promptly encouraged his sister to explore. Philomena was entranced. Without any obvious purpose, Lancelot seemed to have a facet to his body completely absent on her own. She poked and probed. She stuck her nose to it to see if it smelled nice. She sat stock-still, hunting, but the airwaves were beyond comprehension. It seemed completely pointless – no nice smell, no clear aura, no obvious use. Just... there. Perhaps it was detachable. Philomena reached over to test this possibility, taking a firm hold of the thing. At that very moment Parvati descended upon them. She picked Philomena up by the arm and slung her easily onto a broad hip.

'Come,' she said. 'Perhaps God is waiting.'

She carried Philomena across the downs of the golf links, through the wicket gate at the bottom, past the loafers who unfailingly propositioned her every evening and out into the crowded lanes behind the tram terminus.

Philomena was entranced. New smells and sounds rained assault after assault upon her senses. Sweetmeat shop smells, sprinkled with spices, stirred with cow-dung, drizzled with incense. Vendors howling urgently, as though their lives depended on it. Clanging brass and tinkling silver. Insults and exhortations, barking and screeching. This was wonderful! Philomena revelled in the reverberating air. It was a whole new world! Whole lives were floating about these airwaves, and she could see them like others could not because her vision was not distracted by actual sight.

Parvati drove forward through the crowds into the areas that work harder by night. She turned into a shifty lane and ducked into a dark doorway over which hung a dusty yellow board bearing the legend *Dubbal Bullet, Private Club*. Mounting the narrow wooden staircase, Parvati strode down a dim corridor flanked by rows of grilled doors. A few had tired curtains drawn across them; most were empty. In one, two ladies discussed business performances without enthusiam. The smell of cheap perfume and yesterday's ardour hung over the place.

Parvati strode through the corridor to the door at the far end and entered without ceremony. The room was strewn with cheap carpets. Against the far wall was a mattress covered in *zari* quilts upon which a huge woman reclined. Her hair was henna orange, thick, fuzzy and wild. By her side was an ornate brass spittoon. A small wooden cabinet perched on the wall above her head. On its shelves were figures of gods and fake flowers and an electric bulb with a squiggly scarlet filament. The woman picked at the orange cracks in her rotting teeth with an evil-looking poker.

'Aaoo, Parvati,' she said softly, with the soothing, easy tone of the truly deceitful.

'This is the girl I told you about, Zubaidaji,' said Parvati.

The woman waved Parvati closer with the poker.

'Hmm…' she said, pinching Philomena's cheek. Using the grip to turn Philomena's face this way and that, she examined different angles of the child's eyes. She turned abruptly away and directed a stream of orange spittle unerringly into the spittoon. Unravelling her vast bulk,

33

she leaned forward and stared deep into Philomena's eyes. She leaned back against a bolster.

'Child's play,' she pronounced. '*Shabash*, Parvati,' she said, smiling wickedly. 'I will cure her, and she will serve me till she is ready to serve my customers. Agreed?' Parvati nodded.

'Bring me the box by the *almirah*,' said Zubaida.

Parvati watched as Zubaida lay Philomena out under the deity cabinet. Opening the box, Zubaida contemplated its contents for a while. Then she pulled out a glass vial containing a whitish substance that looked like the remains of the night before.

'Lights!' ordered Zubaida with a dismissive gesture, her voice suddenly gruff and distant.

By the light of the orange electric candle Zubaida performed a hundred rituals. She lit incense sticks. She shredded leaves at random. She hummed and whined. The stores in the box seemed inexhaustible. More incense sticks were lit, more leaves shredded. Nuts were ground, the shape of the resultant powder interpreted. Zubaida held the vial up between the palms of her hands and pressed upon it till it shattered. She dropped the mess on the ground and mixed up a concoction with a bleeding hand. She held a dripping finger above Philomena's eyes and waited for a globule to drop into each eye. Then she placed a leaf over the oozing eyes and tied a piece of filthy brocade over them.

Finally Zubaida looked up. 'She must sleep for many hours now,' she said, slipping a medicinal mixture into Philomena's mouth. She saw Parvati's look of surprise at her use of an ordinary sedative.

'It's cheaper,' she said shrugging defensively. 'And more effective.'

Zubaida reached into the depths of her bosom and extracted a bundle of damp money. She peeled off some notes. 'Well done, Parvati,' she murmured. 'The agreed sum was five rupees? Here,' she said holding out the money. 'Now go.'

*

'Where is Philomena?' demanded Hilla of Lancelot.

'Gone to meet God.'

'Stupid boy!' Hilla flung her hands up in exasperation and hurried away to continue her search. An hour later, the recriminations that accompany crises began.

'How could you wait so long without knowing where she was?' demanded Tehmina.

'I can't do everything at the same time,' said Hilla tearfully. 'And I was only away to take the clothes off the line. Five minutes, maybe.'

'Perhaps you should help too, instead of leaving everything to her,' said Edson.

'*You* saying that! What are *you* going to do now?' shrieked Tehmina.

A comprehensive search was launched. Moin joined Edson in the car, his efforts as frenzied as Edson's. They scoured the streets and lanes without reward. Philomena had well and truly vanished.

At ten o'clock, the search was abandoned and the Hill Road police station notified. The officer in charge was sympathetic and assured, and the DaCruzes returned

35

home to their vigil clutching at his confidence. The lights burned all night at the Casa De Familia DaCruz. They sat around the dinner table, the silence broken from time to time by Hilla and Tehmina breaking into tears when a new fear struck their exhausted minds.

The morning brought a visit from the police inspector informing them that every corner in his jurisdiction had been searched without result, and that he had alerted the other police stations in the city. Parvati went about her work silently.

Edson and Moin spent another day ceaselessly prowling the streets and shops, asking questions, receiving no answers. Soon everyone knew that the Casa De Familia DaCruz was missing a child.

As Edson and Moin dragged their way home, Parvati was on her way again. It was Friday, and she knew that most Friday evenings Zubaida would be away entertaining the rich and discreet at the bungalows on Marve Beach. She knew that being Friday evening, chaos would reign in the streets. Slipping in an out of the Dubbal Bullet unnoticed would be easy. She had worked the plan through well, but a cold claw clasped her when she turned into the lane. The Dubbal Bullet seemed deserted, though other houses were frantic with Friday night fever.

'Zubaida's closed today?' she nonchalantly asked a lounging lookout.

'Big job at Powai Lake. Everyone has gone. The pimps are taking the night off.'

If Philomena had been left behind, it would be perfect, thought Parvati. Her heart skipped. What if they had taken Philomena with them? She mounted the steps swiftly. Easing past the dozing minder's room unseen, she ran past the desolate cubicles in the corridor and found Zubaida's door unlocked. Inside, the electric orange candle threw its holy light upon the sleeping figure of Philomena Avan DaCruz.

Philomena had slept the sleep of the dead. She never dreamed anyway: when you have never seen anything, there are no faces or forms to give body to a dream. As Parvati quickly stripped away the cloth over her eyes, Philomena woke drowsily. She rubbed her sticky eyes and noticed something strange. Later, she would learn that it was a colour called Red, like the light from red electric candles. Then a complex moving object came into view. She cried out just as the object put something soft over her mouth, and the next moment she was swung into the air, perched on the object, and moving with it. She closed her eyes and suddenly it became clear. The perch, the gait, the smell. Parvati.

Philomena proceeded to examine this Parvati. There was no scope for imagination or improvisation. It was all so definite, so exact. Philomena was fascinated. Just as she was intently examining Parvati's profile, she found herself in a place filled with other Parvatis, and strange lights and shines and sparkles and darknesses. It was magnificent, and Philomena reached out time and again to touch this world.

You could say that in a way that walk defined Philomena's life – a quest for every experience, to touch as much of the world she saw before her, the belief that happiness was the attainment of only this, that this itself could bring happiness.

*

While the parameters of Philomena's life were being quietly defined on the haunches of Parvati, the DaCruzes were despairingly redefining theirs. The police had come up with nothing. Hilla had prayed hour after hour in her little room at the back of the house till she could speak no more. She sat in a corner of the room, her mind hurling blasphemy at her God. Slowly, bit by bit, the thought crept into her head that Lancelot would need feeding soon. Tehmina, face buried in her pillows, was also finding the same thought peeping through the darkness. Edson had already acted by issuing orders for a meal. The Casa De Familia DaCruz was already adjusting to a world without Philomena.

Outside the gate Parvati was composing herself for the pell-mell rush into the house with Philomena. So far it had gone like clockwork. The only loose end was Zubaida. She would ask around the street, and Parvati must have been seen leaving with Philomena by someone in the crowd. Zubaida would find out, and Zubaida was lethal when crossed. Parvati had had a husband once who had loved a child-woman at Zubaida's and run away with her. They found him in the marshes of the Mahim creek without a face or genitals. The child-woman went back to Zubaida and her delights are still on offer at the Dubbal Bullet. Parvati had no illusions as to her fate if Zubaida's people caught up with her, but she wasn't going to let that happen.

Gathering herself together, she rushed through the gate shouting excitedly. The yelling was joined first by

Sawant in the garden, then Edson from the veranda, and then a disbelieving Tehmina. Hilla rushed out from the kitchens. Perhaps because she had lost her voice, or perhaps because her joy was beyond the reach of any expression, Hilla did not utter a word. She stood in the doorway sobbing silently, watching Edson and Tehmina smothering the child. It suddenly struck her that there was something different about Philomena. Her head, her eyes, moved differently. As the thought mushroomed in her head, Philomena's sight fell on Edson's tiepin, and she reached over to the shiny object. No one realised till suddenly they realised. Hilla leaped forward, whispering as loudly as her throat permitted, 'She can see!'

A fresh wave of arms and lips enveloped Philomena, and this time Hilla joined in. When calm was restored, Tehmina turned to Parvati who had all this time looked on, shedding a tear or two of her own.

'Where was she?' asked Tehmina.

'Roaming around,' said Parvati vaguely.

'Where?' demanded Edson.

'*Juhu*, somewhere.'

'Oh, my poor child! What things you must have been through! What awful places have you been in?' Tehmina pulled Philomena close.

Parvati stepped shyly forward. '*Memsaab*, can I have my salary in advance? The hut needs repair, and a man is coming to repair it....'

Hilla leaned over to Tehmina – domestic affairs were hers to advise on. 'Don't indulge her,' she said. 'She will be getting her pay in a couple of days anyway.'

'I'll give it to you tomorrow,' said Tehmina.

Parvati considered pressing the matter. She knew she could not wait till tomorrow, but Tehmina did not and the offer was clearly reasonable. Quietly, she left.

The night was a long one, suffused with soft warm tears, drenched in happiness. Philomena found the soap bubbles in her bath fascinating, and the sight of her own reflection, and Edson's, and the appearance of a fried *pomfret*, and a million other wonders. A tenderness touched the family that night that made them whole for a few moments, and Edson held Tehmina in his arms as they turned in together in the pale light of dawn.

*

Though the prison-bar windows of Parvati's train to somewhere she watched dawn drawing a golden blanket over the passing hills of Bandra and smiled. She had beaten the dead ends that ruled her life in Bombay and snatched a moment of happiness. She left the city with that hard-earned smile and the remains of Zubaida's five rupees tucked carefully into her blouse.

# *Seven*

Now perhaps this was the sort of thing that makes
fractured families whole again, but a happy symmetry was
not to be. The Empire was under serious siege, and that
meant that life at the Casa de Familia DaCruz was also in
tumult. Edson, whose business was built on an endless
government demand for railway sleepers and an ability to
circulate easily amongst the British civil servants he did
business with, was a man whose true views on the British
Empire made Churchill's seem like those of an Indian
nationalist. And he was not alone. Other great Indian
families were also worried. Meetings were held, at which
shipbuilders and general agents and assorted fat puppies
of the Empire anxiously urged restraint and feared the
consequences of an uprising. They despaired at the
misguided efforts of 'the little bald fellow'. Hours were
spent in oily consultations with British officials, assuaging
their fears and pledging eternal allegiance. Yet everyone

41

could see that the fear and despair were their own. Earning privileges by ingratiation is an arduous process, and the end is unfairly swift. None feared or despaired at the loss of the Indian Empire more than these men; no one grieved more.

'*Arre*, what can happen?' demanded Tehmina. 'They can't take away what we already have. And we *are* Indians. We have rights!'

Sitting side by side on the old chesterfield in the vast living room of Edson's house, Mr and Mrs Marshall nodded in agreement and shifted uncomfortably. Only that afternoon Marshall had been told by his peon at his office in the Registry of the High Court that though *saab* had been good to him, he would have to forget that when the time came. News had filtered through that the native soldiers garrisoned near Nasik had revolted the previous day. The announced court martial had only made matters worse. The city itself was awash with rumours that that morning the Indian soldiers barracked on the eastern side of the Marine Lines had strolled into the British barracks on the seaward side and urinated on the statue of Lord Curzon. Curfews and demonstrations, bombings and beatings were no longer news. Quite irrationally, being jailed had become a matter of pride.

Deep into one melancholy night Mr Marshall, mellow with drink, broke a long silence in the conversation and said with slow finality: 'It is over. We have lost. We have lost because we could not understand that you cannot storm an idea, quell something you cannot actually touch. There is a higher strength that you cannot take guns to. I don't know... maybe we always knew in our

42

hearts that it would happen but never believed you could do it. There is a greatness in your people which will surely send us home one day. But that is not enough, because this sort of greatness retreats to sleep when a crisis recedes. Tackling the ordinary business of life requires a different kind of greatness.'

Marshall rose slowly to his feet, sweeping up his glass of whisky on the way. 'I salute your country!' he pronounced dramatically. Then he sank back into his seat.

'And I fear for it.'

*

'His Majesty's government, being... advised to anticipate the appointed date of June 1948 for the handing over of power in India and the setting up of an independent Indian government or governments, has decided that as from the 15th day of August 1947, two independent dominions shall be set up in India, to be known as India and Pakistan...'

Penelope Bedford, spinster, cat-lover, rose-grower, and long-time resident of Golders Green, London NW11, read over what had just been dictated to her. So this was how you end it, she thought. In a small, slightly smoky room with a few old men sitting round a worn table. Centuries of glory, heroism and foreign graves, all so blandly concluded by a couple of sentences on a small piece of paper.

A few hours later India erupted. In a blaze of utter confusion Tehmina announced to Hilla that they would host a party for freedom and for departing friends on the night of India's independence. Enlisting the services of Mrs Baxter, the Deputy Collector's wife, and Darlington of Peabody & Grimes, Attorneys-at-Law, she set about the business of celebrating a new country and perhaps mourning a little the passing of a way of life.

There were a hundred things to do: the drinks (Darlington), little accompaniments for the drinks (Mrs Baxter), the invitations (Darlington's secretary Sandra Castellino), the music (a reluctant Edson). Then there was the food. Hilla suggested they use Philomena's decisive opinions on food options as a litmus test, but Tehmina, a Parsi to the core, was not going to delegate on this issue. Bipartite conferences of epic gravity ensued between Tehmina and Hilla. The inclusion of *aleti paleti* was agonised over and reluctantly discarded, as much due to Philomena's instantly upturned nose as in deference to the many guests who did not enjoy the pungency of offal. *Sorpotel* was scratched for similar reasons. Included after a mere half-hour deliberation was roast kid, and after a close but tense tussle, *patra ni macchi* sneaked home by a short head from *sali murghi*: Philomena liked 'the colour of the green fish on the white plate', and (pointing at the sea) 'they're so close by!' They briefly discussed the compromises they would need to make in the pungency of the coconut and coriander chutney and moved on to dessert, which was a foregone conclusion – *lagan nu custard*, which Mrs Baxter had on one occasion brightly proclaimed to be 'like crème brûlée'. The analogy had been met by Tehmina with withering contempt. Crème brûlée! A pale and runny-nosed pretender before the emperor of confections!

But the central beauty of the repast could only be Hamidbhai's biryani.

Over the ages millions have been tortured by or have ignorantly drooled over muddled, greasy, congealed masses of *masala* and meat and coloured rice masquerading as biryani. It is a matter of record that the creator of biryani was Khalid, chief chef of the great kitchens of the *Nizams* of Hyderabad. If it is also known that the *Nizams* had decreed that he was to perform his wizardry alone and unassisted, and pass on his knowledge only to a selected person when age destroyed his exactitude with the amount of saffron required. The story that the *Nizams* had from time to time cut off the hands of pretenders who sought to replicate Khalid's work is probably untrue but nevertheless vital to a proper understanding of the art.

At the time Tehmina summoned Hamidbhai it was generally accepted that there were only two or possibly three living exponents of the true tradition: Ghias Miya, the reclusive and irascible master chef of the Karamat Khans of Lahore; Hamidbhai himself, whose knowledge was rumoured to have been gained at the hands of the great Bade Miya himself; and the young Altaf, cook to the royals of Kashmir who, it was rumoured, only tolerated his overt homosexuality because he had evolved a biryani which, though by no means in the classical mould, was sublime enough to be legitimately regarded as a new and exciting school of the classical tradition.

Responding with customary attentiveness to Tehmina's summons, Hamidbhai rolled into the living room, his flushed face beaming. Long years of ingesting only the very finest food had transformed him into a three hundred pound giant, and he winced with the pain from his gout as he lowered himself into a protesting chair without invitation.

'So,' he bellowed merrily. 'A freedom party, and my biryani!' He leaned forward. 'Actually, I was going to make some and distribute it anyway. Now I will make it for your party also, my Freedom Biryani.'

Suddenly struck by his own wit, he bucketed backwards, guffawing. Shaking his head, he wiped the tears from his eyes with the back of his hand.

Hamidbhai warmed to his task. Between copious drafts of fresh lime water, he expounded on the theory of the making of biryani. As always, at a certain stage he veered away towards the dangerous subject of spurious biryani. His outpourings on this topic were legendary and he now set out his stall with gusto.

'Biryani without potatoes!' he exploded. 'Madam, I have had people ask me for biryani without potatoes! And 'littttle more masala', they say! Go find a pimp to cook for you, I tell them! I ask you, how can the flavours of a biryani be put in perspective without the sweet creamy kernel of the potato, fried golden in the finest *ghee*? The potatoes themselves are also important, and one must discard the ones that fall apart before you can run the edge of a fork all the way through them. The ones that do, well... I don't know... throw them away, feed them to the dogs, whatever. And always remember, *maalikan*, that masala is a catalyst for flavour, not an end in itself. Used correctly, properly harmonised, its strength can be harnessed to make magic, but its nature is essentially evil and all-smothering. Once it grabs you, it can be like this,' said Hamidbhai, pointing at a cigarette he had been holding up and waving dramatically as he talked. 'Or *charas*. Or opium. Masala destroys the taste buds, corrodes the sensibilities. How are you going to taste the rice, my long-grained *basmati* beauty? And is the saffron only a colour, or what? And the goat, slaughtered on the precise day, its meat taken only from the inside of the thighs and the marrow bones only from its fore-shanks, did it die in vain? To be brutalised by some son of a whore who wants to hide his uselessness under a fistful of chillies? And do any of these *haraamis* even know that the dough that seals the vessel must have knife-nicks in it, leave aside knowing how deep the incisions should be and at what intervals?' Hamidbhai slumped back into the trembling chair. 'Do you know, there is a restaurant on Lamington Road where they cook the meat and rice separately and throw it together before serving it?' Hamidbhai flung his grand arms up towards the ceiling in despair. Lost in the horror of it, he fell silent.

'What is this great British justice, huh?' he burst out suddenly. 'All sorts of petty fools they have punished, and criminals like these, who should have been the first to be strapped to the cannons at Rampart Row and blown to bits are still nourishing their rotten souls with the money of philistines!' Hamidbhai seemed dangerously close to total apoplexy, and it took several minutes for his vast machinery to revert to something approaching normal. Finally becalmed, a wide smile slowly spread across his face.

'Now let us banish these insects from our minds. A free India shall have a biryani fit for the gods. And when we are free, there will be only little Hamidbhai in the whole country who knows how to make biryani. That madman Ghias in Lahore will be living abroad! He will become a foreigner!' Hamidbhai chuckled to himself at the thought. 'As for that Kashmiri stripling, he is a mere upstart. I am told he washes the rice in lemon milk!' Hamidbhai pondered this for a moment, then snorted derisively. 'Sour touches may waft around the preparation, perhaps from a drop or two of fresh lime at the meal itself, but you cannot build sour flavours into the mixture.'

'Why not?' asked Hilla, who had been listening in from the door.

Hamidbhai turned slowly in her direction, his eyes flashing. 'Because I say so.'

An awkward silence ensued. Then Hamidbhai's eyes twinkled and he began to laugh mightily, shaking the room. When the earthquake subsided to little tremors rippling across his huge frame, Hamidbhai pulled out a handkerchief and wiped his streaming eyes. Suddenly, mid-motion, he stopped.

'The cardamom!' he said to his handkerchief with deadly seriousness. 'The cardamom is too young yet!'

'Sorry,' he said, looking up apologetically. 'Every morning I do a round of my stores, visiting my little ones. Checking their progress, focusing and encouraging the slow ones, scolding the forward ones, discarding the tired ones. You know, that sort of thing. This morning I noticed that the most mature of my five cardamom batches was stubbornly refusing to peak. *Ya Allah!*' Hamidbhai sighed, mopping his face even more furiously.

'Cardamom also matures?' ventured Hilla tentatively.

This time there was no escape. Looming catastrophe had sapped Hamidbhai's humour. He turned imperiously in the direction of Hilla, fixing a steely eye upon her. 'Madam,' he said icily. 'It is mankind's greatest misfortune that most of its food is cooked by disrespectful, ignorant, and slipshod housewives.'

He jumped up with surprising agility. 'Don't worry, I still have a few days to sort this little problem out,' he said, steaming towards the door on the winds of an ideal under siege. As he rolled out, he called out over his or the shoulder, 'Freedom will not wait, not even for my biryani!'

# Eight

For three days and three nights the boy took no food or water. He did not speak or flinch when his father first pleaded with him, then beat him, then tearfully implored him to recant.

On the fourth morning his father woke the boy.

'My son,' he said gently. 'It must be good to have friends like Milton, to love them so much that where they go you must go too, even if it takes you away the whole day and the journey takes longer than its purpose. But spare a thought for me too. God knows that I am with you too little anyway and any one of my absences may turn out to be forever. I miss you so much, but Nestor, my son, you must understand that if I leave you so much and fight and kill, it is because I do it for you, your future, as fathers do in different ways throughout the world. How can I tell you of the pain I feel at every parting, or how I see your face every moment I weaken and feel strong again? And now, your absence when I return will perhaps be too much for this tired old warrior. I know too little about education to understand why you want to go so much, but I too have a little wisdom and I see that you are decided.'

The boy spoke: 'I can go to school with Milton, then?'

His father swallowed hard and nodded.

# Nine

Tehmina and Hilla busied themselves with the preparations for the party. Darlington mooched about the shops, harrying the owners, building a cache of the appropriate wines and champagne and filing periodic progress reports. Mrs Baxter flapped about over the flower arrangements and invitations, despaired at the quality of the ice at the New India Ice Factory on Hill Road, and generally cemented her reputation as an ineffective ditherer. News of Hamidbhai's progress was transmitted by young Rasool, the newspaper boy who slept in the entrance to Hamidbhai's kitchens.

Moin flung himself into the sprucing up of the garden. Every morning he would arrive and promptly mess up something, cheerfully incur the virulent abuse of Sawant, and spend the rest of the day horsing about with Philomena. When it all became too much, Sawant subpoenaed Moin and Philomena and petitioned Tehmina.

'Today's score,' he announced angrily, 'is two flower pots and two flower beds.' He pointed at the guilty pair. Moin was holding Philomena upside down by the ankles as she pummelled his stomach. Both seemed completely unconcerned by the gravity of the proceedings. 'Get them out of the garden or it will look like the third-class compartment of a train to Pakistan. At the journey's end!' Clearly impressed by the studied eloquence of his submission, Sawant whirled around and marched away with a regal toss of the head. Tehmina smiled and went about her business.

Rasool's Biryani Bulletin took a worrying turn for the worse. The previous night, attracted by an almighty clanging crash, the local lads had crept over to its source. Fearfully they looked into Hamidbhai's window and found him practising free kicks on a shiny metal utensil. 'Kicks like Carlton Creado, *yaar*!', Amar the milk boy had said, awestruck. At that moment, Hamidbhai violently jumped on the besieged object, his face contorted with rage. 'Even tackles like Carlton, no?' an increasingly impressed Amar had said. Rasool said there had been a strong smell of cardamom in the air.

The crisis fortunately passed, and the Bulletin returned to reporting more mundane affairs: Hamidbhai's trips to the market, satisfied grunts, strangers at Hamidbhai's house, a night the great man had spent soulfully caressing his cooking implements and reciting sorrowful *shaharis*.

On the morning of the party, the headlines in the *Times of India*, momentous as they were, were dwarfed by the periodical delivered by Rasool. He had been woken early that morning. Not by the tingling feeling that banishes slumber on special days, but by a strange music. The vessels in Hamidbhai's kitchens were singing. He had lain and listened to the symphony: the tap dancing of stirrers on the rims of utensils, the whirling waltzes of great copper spoons upon the bottom of *kadais*. The fanfare of brass mallets on crushing urns, the silky fandango of lids sliding onto bubbling vessels. And over it all, the mesmeric chanting of Hamidbhai coaxing the last drop of flavour from the food. Flailing arms and flying hair, melding his players together, texturising his masterpiece as if there had been no others before or would ever be again. And when the aroma drifted across to him Rasool said he had seen the smoky *dastakhanas* of old Hyderabad and the angels sighing on the rooftops. Later that morning, when Rasool had spoken to others who lived in the lane, they had all said that they had had the same feeling too.

The frenzied build-up to the evening continued. Looking back, Tehmina conceded that there had been far too many people involved. Darlington's obsessive fussiness over how the wines should be stored was an irritant. Sawant's hysterical refusal to snip off a few of his gladioli for the flower arrangement was, in Mrs Baxter's very vocal view, unnecessarily churlish on such an important day. Philomena's enthusiastic investigation of every novelty available drove Hilla to the brink of hysteria, and Lancelot's bovine obsession with the food led to his incarceration in the bathroom for extended periods.

On the mantelpiece Edson's carved-wood clock,

carefully adjusted to the chimes of Big Ben on the BBC, gently ticked away the British Empire. After trying half a dozen positions, Edson had finally decided on the best one for the radio to be placed in. At midnight they would listen in to the programme on the transfer of power and the speeches of the great men of the time.

It was only when Mrs Baxter and Darlington departed to ready themselves for the evening and Philomena and Lancelot were packed off to be cleaned and dressed that peace was restored to the house, and Edson sat down quietly on the veranda to watch India's last British sun slip gently into the same sea over which it had arrived so many years ago.

On that special evening there were many memorable things. Darlington's selection of wines was a sublime riposte to the dark muttering of the city's wine merchants. The coriander and coconut chutney with which Hilla had anointed the *pomfret* was quite majestic in itself. The kid roast had absorbed the flavours of the cashew nuts and cream to perfection. Tehmina had nervously awaited the arrival of the great Freedom Biryani, which was delivered at the very last moment, only just before the kid roast had been served. It was brought out with much fanfare and Carstairs of the Mint – who had had much too much to drink anyway – pretended to swoon in ecstasy after his first mouthful. Other than that there was no humbug chorus of appreciation so prevalent in the polite classes of society, only a stunned silence; the quiet awe that went with humility and disbelief at the levels of perfection a man could actually achieve.

Into this sublime moment came Hilla. She leaned over Tehmina, placing an envelope on the table. 'This came with the biryani,' she said.

'Go on,' said Carstairs. 'The least we can do is see what the maestro has to say.'

'It can wait,' said Tehmina.

But the congregation was in agreement with Carstairs. Perhaps it had something to do with the correct approach to eating the biryani, and that could not wait.

Tehmina hesitated, then opened the letter.

'Respected Tehmina *Begum*,

Herewith the biryani. My Freedom Biryani. I hope it is passable. I have tried as hard as I can, but perhaps it carries in it a drop or two of the juices of sorrow.

This is my home. I am not from Baluch, or the Sindh, or Persia. I am from Bombay, and Bombay alone. But I have had visits from strangers who think otherwise. I have been informed that my home is elsewhere, in a place I do not know and cannot begin to love as home. But these are troubled times, and so by the time you read this I will have left home to go home. See what absurdities are possible in these times!

I must cross a line that has suddenly risen like a twisting serpent from the dust. What awaits me beyond it, I do not know. Anyway, I will not be far away, and I will be writing of my new home to my friends and also to you, Madam. Soon, when all this madness ends I will visit again, and hope to see you visit my home too.

I have rejoiced so much these last few days, lived so much the happiness of our country in its freedom. Now

I grieve just a little about how little happiness our freedom has brought me.

My soul is in this biryani I have made, and perhaps a tear or two. I hope it does not intrude upon the taste. And should you by chance dine after midnight, think of it as a gift from Pakistan.

Ever in respect,
Hamidbhai.'

They sat motionless. The clinking of cutlery had petered out as Tehmina read Hamidbhai's letter, and now the Freedom Biryani turned to ashes.

Edson was the first to break the silence. 'It is almost time,' he said softly. 'I will turn on the radio.'

Now Philomena had always been fascinated by the crackle and pop of the radio, and as they sat waiting for the moment she circled the table, inspecting the device from every angle. She discovered the wire running out from the machine and into the wall. Struck by the apparent untidiness of the offending appendage, its interference with the symmetry of things, she pulled hard at it. It emitted a loud 'phut' accompanied by a spark, and all the lights went out.

Pandemonium reigned. Candles were lit. Help was summoned, and Hilla aimed a swipe at Philomena which she did not seem to mind in the least. A posse of well-meaning impromptu experts converged around the meter-boxes, the fuses, anything that looked vaguely electrical. Carstairs had been spotted inspecting a bundle of knitting wool and muttering that the wiring was 'a ruddy mess'. By the time someone sorted out the problem (more by accident than expertise) the historic moment had passed. Philomena had ensured that history had passed by the Casa De Familia DaCruz.

What had happened in that dark, lost moment? An empire had been lost with some grace. A border appeared, a cook went home. Religion bloodied a country forever. Statesmen smiled and shook each other's hands. Wise men hailed the birth of a nation. Others mourned the murder of it.

\*

You could say that pulling the plug on India's independence was symptomatic of Philomena's approach to life: the unfettered pursuit of experience – it was not the purpose that mattered but the immediate natural requirement to be satisfied. If something demanded investigation it had to be investigated. If something needed to be experienced then the obvious thing to do was to experience it. There was no driven callousness in her actions, no malice in the pain it brought to others. The pain was only her fault in the eye of the sufferer. To her it was merely the logical pursuit of life's many glories – the stroking of beauty, the picking of warts, the stalking of ideas. And sometimes the wilful destruction of the unattainable. But it was always honest, natural and without compromise.

And was she happy on this journey? Did she not hope that one day around the corner she would see what the journey was for? Perhaps she did; certainly she did not think of it. There are things you know and yet are unaware of, and when each day is a quest for snatched experiences and a thousand glimpses of heaven on every passing wind, it has too much in it for you to ponder over yesterday's triumphs or tomorrow's droughts.

While the household had flung itself into the retrieval of the electricity, Philomena had ambled out onto the dark veranda, trying hard to be inconspicuous. It was then that she saw the sky erupt with light. Silhouettes of great ships off the coast flashed silver and grey and red in the light of the dazzling fireworks they launched from their decks. Punched with the design of the wrought-iron veranda railings through which she watched, it was for Philomena one of those images that would waft across her mind from time to time for the rest of her life.

Later, when Philomena asked her mother if she could have a firecracker that made the sky sparkle, Tehmina said no. Later still, when she asked why not, Tehmina said they were too expensive, and that they did not do that sort of thing – it was a Hindu custom, and even they did not set off such absurdly expensive crackers. Philomena wanted to know if the shops kept such crackers and Tehmina said yes. Then someone must be buying them, said Philomena, and Tehmina wearily said she supposed so, adding firmly that they would not be. Philomena put the irrationality of her mother to Hilla, knowing that she seemed to resolve these sort of problems satisfactorily. But Hilla seemed to be sadly uninspired. Repeatedly she said, '*Baap* re! So expensive!' or 'Not our custom.' Philomena resolved her disappointment by deciding that she would just have to steal one for herself.

One evening, as she was being dressed by Hilla for a visit to Hetty Aunty at Tinkerbell Tailors for a trial, Philomena saw her chance. Aunty's shop necessitated a walk past a fireworks store Philomena had seen. Her little mind worked furiously on how to effect the proposed theft till it was halted by their boarding a bus that Philomena knew ran to the Bandra railway station and did not go anywhere near Tinkerbell Tailors. She found the deviation puzzling, but as she was wondering what Hilla was up to she found herself sucked into the sights and sounds and smells of the people around her.

What followed was an hour of quite absurd excitement. The bus journey and the wait at the station were too short for Philomena's sparkling eyes, and the train journey to Santa Cruz was a blizzard of experiences. By the time they alighted from another bus at Juhu Tara, Philomena had completely forgotten about her proposed crime.

They walked down a narrow lane leading onto the Juhu beach, Hilla holding Philomena's hand tight as the girl strained to rush out into the growing expanse of sand and sky and sea at the end of the lane. She sat Philomena down in her lap on a mound of sand on the beach, and together they watched the sun disappear and the sky gather bulk. The last stragglers left the beach. Hilla occasionally said something about a star, or the shape of a cloud, but Philomena was speechless, immersed in the sensual richness of the moment. The wind on her face, its whistle in her ears, the warmth of Hilla's arms and body as she embraced her, the gushing and dying of the twilight waves. A warm, contented shiver flowed down her body.

Hilla set Philomena down beside her. From her shopping bag she pulled out a red canister with embossed golden lettering. Philomena realised immediately what it was.

She stared at it wide-eyed. 'Are you taking it home?' she asked Hilla.

'No,' said Hilla. 'It's yours. But don't tell Mummy, okay?'

Philomena nodded vigorously. She took the object gingerly, staring at it in wonderment, her eyes shining. She turned it around slowly, examining it. Ten rupees! Surely that was much more than what her mother gave Hilla in a whole month? Anyway, it was magnificent! Philomena held it out to Hilla with both hands.

'All right,' said Hilla, reading Philomena's eyes. She led Philomena a little further onto the deserted beach. 'Now sit here and don't move.'

Hilla peered at the instructions in the fading light. Then she moved away some distance and carefully set down the canister on the sand. Shielding the match from the wind, she lit the wick and hurried back to where Philomena was sitting.

A moment or two in every life is touched by the breath of the gods – the kind that stays forever, a safe little cove to pull into in the midst of the jumble of life. It exacts no toll, for to know it is to own it. The fountain flickered silver on Philomena's face, much as a television would one day on the face of an old woman. Hilla's eyes rested softly on Philomena, and for her the beauty of that moment would always be in the look in the little shining eyes. She slipped Philomena's hand into hers and squeezed it. They sat there lost in the moment, on an empty beach with the rustling sea and a sky whose emptiness seemed to weep for its lost blaze of glory.

'Come,' said Hilla when the moment had drained away. 'Let's go home. Quickly now!'

As they walked down the lane Hilla suddenly said, 'What do you say when someone gives you something?'

'Thank you.' said Philomena. She couldn't understand why adults insisted on her saying this even when the words were totally inadequate. Anyway, it was just as well Hilla had resolved this problem, she thought: the firecracker had been far too big for her to have successfully stolen.

From that day on, fireworks evoked no interest in her. Shorn of mystery and distance, they stood vested with ordinariness.

# Ten

Mrs Rispin, Philomena's teacher at Sunningdale Kindergarten, had already noticed this trait in Philomena. The pattern was always the same. She would see something and have to have it. But instead of merely bleating like the other children, Philomena would steadfastly work her way into a position to obtain it. Once attained, there was a ferocious intensity to the process of exploring it and any attempt to interfere was repelled with a viciousness that startled and disturbed Mrs Rispin. When she had unlocked all its secrets and devoured its wonders, she would abandon it without remorse, never to go back to it again. Puzzles, building blocks, snails, earthworms, all suffered the same treatment.

Later, books were to suffer the same fate. She devoured the *Noddy* series, in the simple days before enlightened people decided that children would grow up to be racists by reading them. She devoured her study texts and never returned to them, thus securing for herself the perennial status of a mediocre student. All the while, she read, single-mindedly and obsessively. By the time she was fifteen she had waded through a good part of Edson's library. Austen, Scott, Dickens, Conan Doyle. She discovered way before her time that Brighton Rock was not a part of the fabled English countryside and that Shakespeare was really quite all right. The combination of the attractions of Edson's library and her ephemeral interest in her school texts resulted in her dropping a year at school.

In her final year at school she startled her teacher with her essay on the assigned topic, 'My Religion and its Traditions'.

She wrote:

'Religion is a fraud played upon the illiterate weak by the ignorant but powerful. The only religion is the pursuit of experience. Everything else is somebody else's rubbish.'

0/10, circled for emphasis, with the somewhat dishonest remark: 'This is *not* on the assigned topic. This is *not* an essay.' And most unfairly for that age, the word 'played' had been struck off and corrected to a peevish 'perpetrated'.

Back home in her room that evening, Philomena calmly consulted her dictionary and added 'perpetrate' to her vocabulary.

Leafing through Philomena's notebooks one day, as she did from time to time, Tehmina came across the essay and was more worried than usual. Had she got her hands on those books by that English fellow Russell or something, who Edson had been so taken with recently? She had often told Edson not to let Philomena pick up just anything from his shelf and read it. But the answer was much simpler. It lay in the past, and much closer to home.

*

It was on a Thursday at the end of April in 1953. Philomena had been working herself up towards the thrill of the summer vacations. As always, the rush hour had started on the staircases of her school a minute two or to after the 'home bell' as hundreds of tortured children scampered away from another unwanted day at school.

Philomena descended the stairs two at a time, skilfully negotiated a gaggle of lounging seniors in the compound and jumped into the soft arms of the car. Sawant had accompanied the driver to pick her up, which though not unusual, was an infrequent occurrence. Usually it was Hilla, grumbling about the state of Philomena's clothes all the way home.

'Where's Hilla?' asked Philomena, as she settled down to dismantling the silver window-winder, a project she had inaugurated the day before and which called for speedy completion before it came to the notice of some tiresome adult.

'She hasn't come,' said Sawant.

'Why?' demanded Philomena, which was her question in the first place.

'*Memsaab* will tell you,' said Sawant evasively. Now, 'She's gone to the Fire Temple with *Memsaab*,' or 'She has a cousin visiting' would have done, but there was an uncomfortable quietness in Sawant's voice that swirled across to Philomena and settled uneasily at the bottom of her heart. Something was wrong. Had Hilla left them? Had she collected enough money to start that playschool she was always dreaming about? Was she ill?

'Where has she gone?' asked Philomena fearfully, a little frantically.

Sawant looked straight ahead. 'She is... starting at a new place,' he said.

Impossible, thought Philomena. Hilla would never leave her. Ever.

It was then that she realised that they were not on the road home.

'Where are we going?' she asked.

'Oh, I have to order some manure on the way home,' said Sawant vaguely.

The drive went on and on, the streets becoming more and more unfamiliar. They were distant, foreboding, confusing. Something was happening, and no one was telling her. They swept down street after street, round corner after corner. A last right turn and they entered an imposing gate with huge glass lampshades in the shape of the holy Parsi fire on either side. This place she knew and remembered. The Towers of Silence. Death. If something horrible had happened and she was to be brought here from school, Hilla would have come and not Sawant. As they drove up the winding road through the woods on the hill where the funeral houses

66

were, she knew. Hilla was dead. Hilla had left her. Forever.

Before the car could come to a standstill she had flung open the door and leaped out. She saw her father sitting on a wooden bench outside one of the bungalows and her mother standing inside the door. She pelted forward. As she reached the steps to the bungalow, Edson rose quickly and scooped her into his arms. He held her tight to him and whispered 'No darling, only Parsis can go in. We are not allowed.'

From over Edson's shoulder Philomena could see into the dim, firelit room. In the centre was a white bundle on a cot. So small. So... ended. She saw Hilla's face. It was different, somehow far away. There, but gone. She saw the fire flash and jump in the eyes of the rustling white-cassocked priests. Their beards trembled as their voices bounded about the room. A dog was led in.

As it passed them, Philomena asked Edson 'He is a Parsi?' Edson smiled and said nothing.

The ceremony ended. As the pallbearers brought the cot out they asked Edson move away. Pairs of mourners formed a train behind the cot, each pair holding opposite ends of a handkerchief.

'Mama,' called Philomena from Edson's arms. 'Mama, please, can I touch her just once?'

Tehmina went over to the priests.

'Out of the question,' said the head priest. 'None can now defile the body, much less someone from without the faith.'

The procession began to move up through the small floral arch beyond which lay the flower-ridden path to the gaunt walls of the *dakhma*, the central well where the body would be left exposed to the beady attentions of the vultures.

Edson put Philomena down. Unravelling his handkerchief, he gave one end to Philomena. Holding the other end himself, they joined the procession. When the reached the arch, a muslin-vested priest held out a beefy arm.

'Sorry *sahib*, but you are not permitted beyond this point.'

Philomena watched frantically as the bobbing cot receded in the distance. Suddenly she realised that she would never see Hilla again.

'No!' she screamed in panic. Twisting out of Edson's grasp, she flew forward, but the Muslin Vest grabbed hold of her. She kicked and wailed, straining every tiny sinew in her body. Between them Edson and the priest only just managed to quell the assault. When she tired, they relaxed their grip and she suddenly twisted out and ran away. She ran past the parked cars, down the mossy, wooded road toward the gates. She may have stumbled, fallen, gashed herself – she didn't notice. Edson and a startled Sawant followed in hot pursuit. They screamed to the gatekeeper to stop her, and he reacted swiftly, lifting her off her feet and sitting her down on a mossy boulder by the gate. When Edson arrived, breathless and shaking, she looked up at him through her little wet eyes.

'Why!?' she cried out. It was a broken and piteous sound, ruptured by a hundred different agonies. Edson paced up and down beside her, gasping for breath, searching for an answer.

Dusk fell as Edson and Philomena sat on the boulder, grappling quietly with their confusions. The gatekeeper sat on the steps of his hut, staring into the distance. But for an occasional sniffle from Philomena or a slow, sad shake of the head by Edson, they could have been statues.

Then the gatekeeper rose slowly to his feet and shuffled into the hut to switch on the lights. The holy fires shone bright over the gateposts. Philomena looked up slowly at them, her lips twitching, rivers of tears shining on her cheeks. She reached over to a pebble and hurled it at a holy fire lampshade with all her might. A piece of glass fell to the ground. The lamp shone on, tainted but unmoved.

The gatekeeper came to the door of the hut and saw what happened.

'This will be trouble for me,' he said, scratching his stubble.

Edson turned and looked at him. 'Don't worry, I'd be delighted to pay for it – I'll make sure it is put on the bill,' he said, smiling grimly to himself.

The piece of broken glass glinted in the light. Philomena went over and picked it up. It looked like a star. She slipped it into the pocket of her pinafore. Then she looked up at the blighted holy fire once more and turned and walked away.

Much later that night, Edson and Tehmina sat on the little bench outside the funeral bungalow where relatives and close friends would keep vigil and have prayers recited for the departing soul for the next four days and nights. A naked bulb hung over the entrance to the

69

bungalow, adding its morose, sorry hue to the scene. Frogs burped in the cool darkness. The trees in the woods whispered. Somewhere in the distance in some other bungalow the White Cassocks heralded someone else's pain. Edson shifted uncomfortably, tossing questions to the night.

Finally he turned to Tehmina. 'She only wanted to touch her!'

Tehmina shook her head, as though the decision was beyond question.

Edson looked away. He leaned back and threw his head up, gazing into the night. Softly, to no one in particular, he said: 'How can an act of love be blasphemy?'

*

Perhaps if Tehmina had remembered that night while reading through Philomena's essay years later she would not have turned on Russell so readily.

# Eleven

'Horrorshow groodies!' said Philomena, lifting her eyes from her book and staring evenly at Ala Aunty's ample bosom.

Philomena's aunt Alamai was visiting (as she did periodically) and overstaying her welcome (as she did unfailingly).

She turned to Philomena. 'I beg your pardon?'

'Horrorshow groodies,' repeated Philomena, pointing at Alamai's chest.

Alamai's eyes flustered around the room and settled on Tehmina. 'What is she talking about?'

Philomena smiled insolently. She had been reading in the old easy chair by the window that opened onto the veranda. Slowly unwinding herself, she got up and sauntered away to her room, book in hand.

'That girl is going to be a big problem, dressed like that,' Alamai said disapprovingly as she watched the easy roll of Philomena's behind and the jounce of her breasts beneath the loose, flowing shirt. 'I mean, you can't blame the boys, can you?'

'As far as I can see,' said Tehmina resignedly, 'she doesn't see any problem arising at all. With this girl, when she wants something she just goes and gets it. And boys seem to be something she wants from time to time.'

Alamai looked horrified. 'You mean...'

'I mean that she does exactly what she wants and I cannot understand her. What does "horrorshow groodies" mean, for example? Must be from that the book she is reading. I took a look at yesterday. It doesn't even seem to be in English. And there is nothing in her education which would allow her to understand it and not me. I just don't know.' She fell silent.

'*A Clockwork Orange*!' She saw the confusion on Alamai's face. 'That's the name of the book,' she said, in a slightly condescending tone. 'And lately the music she's been listening to... *baap re*! She used to listen to Edson's music, Beethoven and all. But nowadays she brings home all this modern stuff by people with strange names. She shuddered theatrically, driving home the gravity of the situation. 'Of course, she still listens to Edson's music, but much less. And you know, she goes to college and comes back with her clothes smelling of tobacco, and sometimes they smell of tobacco but not ordinary tobacco. She must be sitting with some friends who smoke hookahs or something!'

Alamai's gulped, her eyes wide with horror.

'What am I to do?' continued Tehmina. 'And how can you say it is my fault? Look at Lancelot. Such an honest and hard-working boy. Quiet, well-behaved. And then this hellfire!' she said, waving in the direction of Philomena's room.

Alamai frowned in puzzlement. 'Where does all this come from? Edson is a level-headed person, and though you were a little impetuous earlier, that was only your youth, not you.'

Tehmina shifted uncomfortably. 'Edson thinks anything his children do must be right for them, so he won't interfere. And me, if I tell her what is right it only convinces her it isn't.' Tehmina fell silent for a moment before starting again. 'And the way she comes and goes! In this moment, out the next. And lately she has taken to staying out till quite late at night. All sorts of boys drop her home! I just had to talk to Edson about it, and all he said was that there was nothing she could do at night that she could not do by day and it was no point worrying about it. Now *you* tell me what to say!'

With exemplary timing, Philomena streamed out of her room, flung a casual farewell in the direction of Tehmina and Alamai and carried on towards the door.

'Where are you going, dear?' asked Alamai.

Philomena noticed the hint of a challenge in her aunt's tone and the rage rose within her. She turned around, smiling sweetly. 'To have sex.'

She gave herself a moment to enjoy Alamai's impersonation of a traumatised goldfish and left.

Well, it was true, actually. A few weeks ago she had had one of those afternoons that people have the minute their parents leave town. Long, lazy, hash-stained hours spent sprawled over a devastated house, someone trying to convince Guru that there was an intangible flabbiness to Led Zeppelin, someone else trying to convince Lefty that there was a divine tautness to Nietzsche.

It was during one of those sessions that she found herself resting her head on Arun Palitkar's thigh as he manfully struggled through a particularly awful rendition of 'Hard Rains A-Gonna Fall' on his battered and stubbornly tuneless guitar. A drowsy sexuality hung about the room. Philomena had been vaguely contemplating getting herself fucked for a while now. She threw her arm back over her head, and rested it on Arun's leg. Idly, she began to run it up and down along his thigh. Slowly, his singing faded. They sat like that a while, letting the mood envelope them. Then Arun leaned forward and their half-closed eyes met. They got up and wandered off into another room, where they had sex.

What? Had sex? Just that? Had sex? No delicate fluttering of hands and hearts? No trembling emotions? No explosions of heart-shaped stars? No gentle nuzzling of Arun's bare, brown chest? No satisfied sighing into tremulous breasts? No emotional wrench at the loss of innocence? Well, no. Philomena had discovered a new passion, and she had no time for all that. She had broken into a new world. A new dimension of her senses, completely divorced from the world around it. No baggage. No Nietzsche. No Zeppelin. No droogs. No Arun Palitkar. Sex.

When it was over, Arun, ever the sensitive poet, tenderly asked her if she was okay. She looked at him beaming broadly and said she was fine. Then she jumped up, bent over and kissed his subsiding erection, and pulled on her trousers.

'I've got to take a piss. See you outside.'

Arun lay there staring at the ceiling for while. Then he slowly got up and fished about for paper and pen and wrote a poem.

\*

'The essential thing,' said Jesus Kurien, pulling hard at a *chillum* the size of an ice-cream cone, 'is positioning.'

Jesus was balanced precariously on the iron railing that protected the little garden outside the college from the bourgeois realities of formal education that washed about its borders. It wasn't that the inmates of the infamous Garden of Eden were illiterates or philistines – Jesus himself would in later years spend his time teaching the intricacies of nuclear physics to students up and down the Western world. 'Ziggy' Fatehally, (so named because Jesus, her mentor and occasional lover, had decided that she was '*hazaar* androgynous'), would later occupy senior positions in the World Bank. And there were future historians, social philosophers, scientists, alternative strategists, and even (heaven forgive them) business wizards in attendance at that shrine of knowledge and excess. Well-lubricated by a steady flow of *chai* from the canteen, and hashish from the cigarette-wallah behind the Regal Cinema, the Garden of Eden was a higher institution, attracting only those who had transcended the pettiness of grades and rank. Their education was effected in somewhat unconventional ways: they watched the stunning efficiency of the cigarette-wallah's distribution and delivery systems and spent days debating whether illegality raises the efficiency levels of enterprise. This inevitably led to a furious debate over whether conformation with the law stunted initiative and growth. It was a good education, though the faculty seemed to consider them heretical wastrels.

'Positioning,' repeated Jesus, ' is everything. You see, when I board the train in the morning I must anticipate the conditions I am likely to encounter – who is around me, what they are like. Avoid the chaps with briefcases – once they are safely on they tend to just drop them in the general direction of where they think the floor must be, completely ignoring the possibility that that there may be someone's feet in between. Also, look around for polyester shirts. The body odour on polyester shirts is nature's revenge upon the industrial age. It's not so bad if the chaps wearing them are leaning against the side, or holding onto the vertical bars. But God help you if you find yourself next to a Polyester Shirt that is holding onto the overhead straps. And he is probably the same fuck who smiles patronisingly at you when he sees you are reading *The Economic and Political Weekly*. Then you have to work out as to which side of the train the next station's platform will be on, and the next, and the next, all the way to Churchgate, because a minor miscalculation could find you on your bum amongst the cow dung at the next station.'

Jesus took another drag at his exotic ice-cream cone, frowned because it had gone out, lit it messily, dropped his chin onto his chest and shook his head slowly. 'It is all positioning. Always positioning. Look at the guy who kept pushing the stone up the hill and every time he almost got to the top he lost control and it rolled all the way back.' He shrugged and opened his palms out to the sky. 'Same thing. No positioning.'

Jesus noticed that his expansive gesture had tipped the contents of his *chillum* onto the grass. He spent the next few minutes scrambling about on the ground, trying to shovel the smoky mess back into his *chillum*. Abandoning the attempted recovery, he drew himself up and pulled out a colossal clump of hash from his trouser pocket. 'See? No problem. You have got to make sure that your position covers the possibilities. You won't ever find me without a good stone, like that fuck on the hill did!' He chuckled quietly at his humour.

'Sisyphus,' said Philomena with lazy superiority.

'What?'

'The name is Sisyphus,'

Jesus smiled at her. 'You know your problem Phil? You have a bourgeois eagerness to show off whatever pitiful knowledge you may happen to possess.'

It was at this point that Arun Palitkar arrived. He sat down heavily, and stuck out his hand for Jesus's *chillum*. 'They wouldn't accept it. That silly stuffy bitch Guzdar wouldn't accept it. And I've seen the crap that they have!'

Giselle jumped in. 'Look, did you seriously expect us to publish that poem of yours?' she said.

'Why not?' snapped Arun. 'Are you saying you don't like it? Are you saying it's not good enough? You saying you have better stuff?' he challenged.

77

'Look, *I* quite like it. But that's not the point,' said Giselle.

'Why not? You're the fucking student editor. She's only the... principal... staff... editor. You could have pulled for it. It's bloody brilliant.'

'Well, I would have, except that I know that the only way for it to get published is to change it around a bit, and you're too screwed up in the head to understand that your art cannot be appreciated if no one gets to read it. I mean, did you really think you could get a poem called "The First Fuck is the Deepest" past Guzzler? Or that I'd pull for something with a corny, borrowed title?? And anyway, who the hell cares about the details of your artistic explosions on top of Phil!' said Giselle, who quite fancied Arun herself.

'Forget about them,' said Philomena, patting Arun's shoulder gently. 'You just keep doing what feels right to you.'

'Your people back yet?' Jesus asked Arun.

'No,' said Arun sulkily.

'Good. Let's go.'

Back in the chaos of Arun's house, Philomena felt Arun's aching gaze upon her. He came over to her and asked if she wanted to go to his room.

Philomena leaned back and held up her hand. 'I'm fine,' she said lazily.

At some stage that afternoon, Philomena followed Jesus out of the room and led him to Arun's room. A while later, Arun followed the sounds of Philomena to his bedroom door.

78

He hesitated, then knocked. 'I've snapped a guitar string. I need to get some from my drawer,' he called out casually.

'Hang on a second,' gasped Philomena from behind the door. 'We're not finished yet.'

# Twelve

'In your own hands! The power to fly! Fly a helicopter with the power in your hands!'

It was a rich, deep voice, strong and full of life. Philomena was walking on the pavement outside the Prince of Wales Museum, mulling over her decision not to sit the examinations this time round.

'Learn from a magician from Africa how to fly a helicopter made in Japan! Aha! Miss! Only five rupees! Five rupees to fly!'

Philomena turned to look. Sitting on the pavement was a huge jute sack and next to it an array of the most hideous coloured plastic helicopters. Behind them bounced two bright, laughing eyes in a dark face on a dark body which swayed easily from side to side under a purple bush shirt. He was younger than his voice. She glanced over the stall. Lying on top of the jute sack was an ancient copy of the first volume of Johnson's *Lives of the English Poets*. Philomena was intrigued.

'Is that yours?' she asked, pointing to the book.

'Yes, madam,' he said brightly.

'And is it also for sale?'

'No, no, that is mine.'

'Well, it is the only thing worth buying,' said Philomena.

'Miss, you are very rude to a foreigner in your beautiful country. I am a humble student in need of the money, and it makes me feel good to stand here in the sun and watch the world trying to ignore me. Only the children talk to me, because they do not judge me without even speaking to me!'

He picked up a pink helicopter. 'Want to try? I guarantee it will be more fun than *Tess*,' he said, smiling and pointing at the book sticking out of Philomena's bag.

She looked for a moment at his smiling face. Then she walked around the helicopters to where he was standing and dumped her things on the pavement.

'Phil DaCruz,' she said, sticking out her hand.

'Phil,' he repeated. 'Mmm. I am Nestor Musambe.' Turning away, he picked up a helicopter. 'Now, this is how you do it. All you do is pull the serrated plastic strip through the cogged hole in the central spindle and release the catch.' Philomena watched the helicopter proceed on its elegant but random way. Nestor retrieved the helicopter from where it had come down and went back to work.

'Oi! Lady, Gentle-man. Latest from Japan! Aviation technology in your hands! Helli-copters! Helli-copters!

Five rupees! Only five rupees!' He glanced indulgently at Philomena, who was eagerly testing helicopter after helicopter and taking bets with herself as to where they would land.

Philomena carefully inspected the tiny label on the helicopters and discovered that 'Japan' was a building called Japan Co-operative Housing Society in Thana, on the outskirts of Bombay.

Sales were fairly brisk that afternoon, and the only customer that Nestor lost was the one he had to abandon to retrieve a helicopter released by Philomena which splashed down on Bholanath the sugar-cane juice seller's glasses. The afternoon flew by Philomena and Nestor. At the end of the day they sat next to each other on the pavement, resting their backs on the cool stone of the museum walls as Nestor did the accounts. Philomena closed her eyes and re-lived the sun-dappled flights of helicopters, the laughter in Nestor's eyes, and the camaraderie of the shirt sellers and the junk hawkers who didn't make much but made it happily.

'What is all this, then?' said a crisp, authoritative voice.

Philomena opened her eyes. In front of her was a boy, not yet ten. Hands on hips, he was addressing Nestor directly and purposefully.

'And who is the *ladki*?' he demanded, pointing a finger at Philomena without shifting his gaze from Nestor.

'A friend,' Nestor mumbled. 'She's just helping.'

Philomena turned sharply to Nestor, startled by the fluency of his Hindi. She pointed an equally insolent finger at the boy. 'Who's the kid?' she asked.

'Umm... this is Kailash,' said Nestor. 'We are sort of... partners, but running different businesses. There are a couple of others too. Kailash sort of... handles... the overall administration of the syndicate.'

Kailash had in the meantime turned his attentions to Philomena, inspecting her thoroughly. Finally he turned back to Nestor. 'Sexy,' he pronounced. 'Always a double-edged weapon. Anyway, you seem to have sold more than usual.' Then he frowned to himself. 'Difficult things, women. Be careful.'

Philomena smiled at Kailash. 'And what is your chosen line of work?'

Kailash eyed Philomena suspiciously. Turning to Nestor he asked, 'Are you sure she is not a police informer? Why does she ask so many questions?'

Kailash screwed up his face, considering the position. 'All right, I'll tell you. But you're obviously rich, so you have to buy us *chai* first.'

Philomena plonked herself down in the tube-lit comfort of the Café Royal and pressed her palms to the cool marble top of the little round table. Kailash hoisted himself onto a chair, planted his elbows on the marble top and barked out an order for three *gulabi chais*.

'You see,' he started, 'I have a mechanical background, so the natural thing to do is to use my expertise.'

'For crime,' growled Nestor into his chin.

Kailash gave Nestor a pained look and then continued smoothly. 'You may have noticed that these new cars that people like your father seem to be buying these days run on petrol. The petrol goes from the petrol tank to the engine through a pipe which runs all the way down the left underside of the car. Now the amazing thing is, those *gaandus* in Europe designed a car with a joint halfway down the pipe which can be easily disconnected.'

'You disconnect petrol pipes for a living? That must pay well!' said Philomena archly.

Kailash slapped his forehead and looked at Nestor. 'Now do you understand why I keep telling you that women are a useless time-pass?' He turned back to Philomena. 'Madam,' he said with exaggerated politeness, 'the petrol flows through a pipe to something called a carburettor, which holds a little petrol and feeds it to the engine. My job is to lounge about at traffic signals, drop out of sight, wriggle between waiting cars, and undo the pipe at the joint. What is your name?'

Philomena started and told him.

'Mr DaCruz,' continued Kailash without missing a beat, 'proudly driving his new car, proceeds from my signal using the fuel already in his carburettor, which carries him between 380 and 400 yards down the road before it runs out.'

'You sound more like a vandal than a mechanic,' said Philomena.

'So much money, and still no brains! When the car finally runs out of petrol my associate is on hand to render assistance to Mr DaCruz who of course knows nothing about the mechanics of the car he is driving. It helps if it is raining, but at worst we make five rupees from each car.' Kailash paused and scratched his chin reflectively. 'Trouble is,' he continued, 'the *saala* police are getting smart. Sorry, not smart, that's impossible.' But you know, someone must have very slowly explained to them how the operation works and they seem to be lurking about at all the usual junctions – Haji Ali, Metro, Flora Fountain, those sort of places.' He turned to Nestor. 'It is something I want to bring up at the next meeting.'

'Show me how,' said Philomena suddenly.

Kailash looked at her as though she was mad. 'You see, in certain lines of work, like Nestor's for example, someone like you can be of some use. But in my field you would not get a moment away from the attentions of the police. Trust me, there is no future in street crime for the sexy ladies of Bombay.'

Kailash hopped off his chair. 'Salaam!' he said, saluting jauntily. As he walked briskly towards the exit he grabbed a handful of the digestive sweets that the owner kept on his counter for respectable paying customers. Neatly ducking the proprietor's incensed swipe at his head, Kailash shot out into the crowds and disappeared.

Philomena smiled. 'So tell me,' she said. 'Is selling helicopters all you do in life?'

Nestor looked embarrassed. 'Actually, I'm studying. That is the reason I came here. Second year BA, economics and politics. But you probably know that we have problems back home, and I need to pay for things. Life costs, and there is never enough.' He frowned. 'Funny thing is, someone here sends me a little every month, and I have never been able to find out who. A few rupees in the post, at my hostel – just enough to 'cover the fees and the room charges. I wish I knew who was sending it – not to return it, but maybe if I could just thank them...'

Philomena had no time for the appreciation of charity. 'So tell me about your country. It's the Russians and the Americans again, isn't it? Another away game in Africa.'

'Well, there is a thug who has declared himself president for life, and he is supported by the Right. And there is the rest of the country that wants him out and the Russians conveniently see their point of view. Maybe the government gets a little support from the Americans, but not much because we have nothing of value to them, except perhaps a little tin. Not enough to make it really important to either. Anyway, I left four years ago. Or rather, I was sent. I don't know who arranged it, but it couldn't have been my father – he never had enough. An uncle perhaps. I don't know; I never tried to find out.'

'If you came here four years ago why are you still in your second year at college?' asked Philomena.

Nestor looked down again. 'When I first came it was hard. Everything was hard – the language, the work, the money, being alone. I failed. It happened again the next year. Now I have some money from the helicopters and things, and friends also – Kailash, the others, so I am not alone any more. But I will probably fail again this year.'

'Why is that?'

'When you finish your course you have to return home. I am only allowed to stay because I'm studying here.' He hesitated. 'Most of the time I write poetry,' he confessed shyly.

'What about?'

'Home. Laughter. Violence. Flowers. The savannah, and the colour of the evening sun on it. Childhoods. Happiness. Pain. Regrets....' His voice trailed off as the poet in him that had unexpectedly surfaced subsided, and his eyes snapped back to the present. 'And you,' he asked. 'Have you finished at university? What next? Oxford? Cambridge? Isn't that where all of you go to join the club and let your hair down for a bit? Where will you be going?'

'Can I read them, your poems?'

Nestor shook his head firmly. 'So where will you be going?'

Philomena leaned back and smiled. 'Africa, perhaps.'

As they pushed their way through the evening rush they said nothing, revelling in each other's presence. They reached the side entrance to Churchgate station, across the road from which stood Nestor's hostel. Philomena pushed her way through to a corner at the side of the concourse. Turning to Nestor she suddenly leaned forward and kissed him quickly on the cheek. 'I don't need to go anywhere to let my hair down,' she said smiling. Then she turned and wafted away into the homing crowds.

It was all really very simple and natural. Nestor continued to hawk his wares at his pitch outside the museum and Philomena continued to stroll by the same spot. At the end of the week she had drunk a lot of cheap tea, harried Nestor to let her read what she called his 'Nostalgia' poems without success, closely scrutinised Kailash's traffic-signal contortions, and kissed Nestor properly outside his hostel to a chorus of appreciative cheers from loitering inmates.

On a warm orange evening in June, Nestor was introduced to Tehmina on the veranda of the Casa de Familia DaCruz.

'This is Nestor,' Philomena said matter-of-factly. Then as she turned away she added loudly, as if to herself, 'Whose colour is going to test her.'

'Such rubbish you talk!' said Tehmina nervously. 'Come on in, dear,' she said, putting out a guiding hand but not actually touching him. 'And where did you meet my impossible daughter?'

Nestor was about to explain when Philomena called out to him from a distant passage to follow her to her room. Tehmina's brow furrowed for a second, then cleared. 'Go ahead, dear,' she said sweetly.

They had barely settled down in Philomena's room when Tehmina appeared at the door. 'Would you like some tea?' she asked.

'Yes, please,' said Nestor. Philomena nodded a curt assent.

Moments later Tehmina came in again. 'Tea is ready: the water was on the boil already!' she said brightly.

'We will have it here,' said Philomena brusquely.

'Oh, but I...'

'Whatever is more convenient to you, ma'am,' said Nestor, drawing a dark look from Philomena.

'Well, it would be nice if we could sit out on the veranda. We have some nice pastries as well. Come along,' she said, turning away.

Philomena glared at Nestor as they made their way to the veranda. 'Stupid polite fuck!' she hissed.

The conversation between Tehmina and Nestor was

strained. Philomena gracelessly shunned the proceedings, taking it in turns to glower at Nestor and her mother, make withering comments, and carry out a detailed analysis of the state of the crockery. She noticed that the teapot handle was not aligned properly, the flowers on the saucers had faded unevenly, and Nestor's cup was chipped at the base. Her interest in the ongoing conversation extended to looking for occasions to put the boot in.

'I have to go into town now,' said Tehmina finally. 'Perhaps you would like me to give you a lift back to your hostel?'

'Er....'

'No thank you,' finished Philomena. 'He will be taking a train back later.'

'Oh, I am not in any hurry. We can leave whenever you are ready.'

Philomena gritted her teeth. 'Let's leave then. I am going back too, so you can give us both a lift.'

In the hope that familiarity would eventually breed indifference, Philomena brought Nestor home regularly. One evening, again outmanoeuvred into sitting on the veranda for tea, she resumed her examination of the crockery and noticed that Nestor was drinking from the same chipped cup she had noticed earlier. Then it happened again the next time, and the next. Seething inside, she waited patiently till one day Nestor asked for more sugar in his tea.

She swooped down on his cup. 'Swap – I've put too much in mine.'

'No, no dear,' said Tehmina hastily. 'There is plenty more. Just make yourself a fresh cup.'

Philomena wagged her finger at her mother in mock disapproval. 'Waste! My mother always told me to never waste things.' She drank down the tea before Tehmina could react.

# Thirteen

Finally one day, quite by chance in Nestor's eyes and by tortuous device to Philomena's knowledge, they did find themselves alone together.

It was a magical afternoon. Through the huge windows in Philomena's room the sun streamed over their nakedness and Philomena moved and cried out with emotions that surprised and confused her. As they lay together afterwards, she felt Nestor's head shaking gently from side to side on her breast. Looking down, she saw a strange smile playing on his lips.

'What?' she asked softly, gently scratching the back of his neck.

'I didn't think girls in India did this sort of thing!' he said, still smiling.

Philomena sat up abruptly. Pushing him away, she stood up, her naked body shining angrily in the evening sun. 'Do pigeons mate on the rafters in India? Do dogs rut in the open in India? Do men wear trousers in India? Are there whores in India, and do married men go to them? Do women have affairs here? Do Indians actually fuck or do the storks bring them their babies?' She smiled a humourless smile. 'How can you be so bloody illiterate!'

Nestor smiled sheepishly. He hooked an arm around her thighs and pulled her to him, and this time she tore him to shreds.

'I'm sorry,' she said afterwards. 'It's just that... I mean, are our temple carvings the work of westerners? Did the *sadhus* learn about hashish and opium from the hippies?' She ran the back of her fingers gently across an angry scratch on the back of Nestor's neck. 'We taught the world how to dope and fuck, and now we desperately try to make the world forget it, trying so hard to become the smallest people of all, frantically scraping together this veneer of rectitude to cover for our suddenly shameful past!'

'Sorry I spoke!' said Nestor.

They lay together silently for a while. Then Nestor suddenly jumped up. 'Damn! I'm later for my meeting. Want to come? You can't actually attend it, but maybe I can get you into my room later.'

'What meeting?' asked Philomena.

'FOSEPA,' said Nestor.

Philomena's pursed her lips. 'What, pray,' she asked testily, 'is FOSAPA?'

'FOSAPA. The Foreign Students' Academic Progress Association. I've just passed my exams, so I will obviously be a major topic at the meeting. We usually hold it under the gulmohar tree in the hostel compound. Want to come? There are plenty of loiterers around anyway, so you can just hang around.'

By the time they arrived the meeting was already in progress. Philomena looked around. She recognised the Iranians Mahirnosh and Bahram. Sitting next to them was Ntini from Central Africa, and beside him Hasan, Salima and Shamin, who were Iraqis. She waved cheerfully to Tikoy of Tanzania who was sitting with a group of students she couldn't place offhand.

Looking around the congregation, the inclusion of the words 'Academic Progress' in the association's name seemed violently inappropriate: Nestor's success at the examinations should have been a rare moment of riotous celebration. But Nestor's appearance at the meeting only brought forth a muted murmur and Philomena was sure she heard a couple of voices mutter, 'Sorry, maan' as he sat down.

Mahen the Mauritian, started to speak. Philomena knew him from her Pope tutorial batch as being a mysterious amalgam of brilliance in class and utter uselessness in examinations.

'See Nestor, maan,' said Mahen, 'the problem is that you are confused. Most of us know what we want, which is not to have to go back home. Everything has to be planned with that in mind. I mean, passing is easy – every fool passes here. The real skill is in passing at the right *time*, which is just before you get chucked out for good. And when is that?'

Murmurs all round of 'Three years max. in one class, maan.'

Mahen pointed a reiterating finger at Nestor. 'Every year, year after year. Timing. Judgement. One slip and you are through. Take Mahirnosh here. A fool!' Mahirnosh squirmed uncomfortably under the scornful gaze of the congregation. 'Finished off a four-year course in eight. Has to now depend on a Masters, or more accurately, hope they let him do one, considering he took eight years to get an undergraduate degree.' He leaned back and gazed at Mahirnosh. 'So chances are that this time next year our friend Mahirnosh, our ace centre-back, will be back home. So when the Shatt-al-Arab Party starts he'll be lobbing grenades at Hasan's people and hoping that they are as incompetent as his friend Hasan back in Bombay, *who*, it must be admitted, has judged his failures to perfection.'

He turned again to Nestor. 'What were you expecting? A fucking citation? The trouble with you is that your nerves don't hold at the vital juncture. Failing requires nerves of steel, an unshakeable belief in your ability to push through at the last possible attempt. There is no margin available. You *must* fail till the last permissible moment, because the difference is a whole year, and a year can make the difference between being alive in this country or being dead in your own.'

'Maybe it's just that I am not terrified about going home,' muttered Nestor defensively.

'Home? *Home*??' Mahen frowned with mock concentration. 'Let's see, now. Who is it at the moment, the communists or the fascists?' That's it! It's the fascists! And has your father started a little business which is coming along very nicely, thank you? And does he pour antiseptic over his shiny new shoes as he steps over the bodies in the streets on his way to work? And is everyone dead pleased with the money they are saving by hiding it away from the thugs in government so that it can be taken away later by the thugs in the rebel forces? And will your father come home tonight chuckling happily about his business, or will one or other of the thugs butcher him in some dark lane for being happy at all?'

Mahen stopped for breath. In the silence, Nestor softly said: 'They did. And he was not even happy.'

There was an awkward silence. Then the discussion ran away and hid behind instructions to so-and-so to submit blank papers at the preliminary examinations, to someone else to turn up in the afternoon for an examination scheduled for the morning. As the meeting broke up, Mahen patted Nestor's arm as he passed and mumbled an apology. Nestor nodded slowly to him.

*

'When did he die?' asked Philomena as they sat under the dreary light bulb among the dirty green walls and wank-sodden air of Nestor's hostel.

'I don't know. It was after I had left. I received a letter from Milton – he is from my village, my oldest friend. Closer than blood. Anyway, Milton wrote and said that Pa had had an argument with a colleague in the movement. The rebel movement, that is. Everyone seems to be something in the rebel movement, unless they are getting handouts from the government to be spies. The rebels are supposed to be communist-funded, and I suppose they are, if you can call it funding. Most people don't really care about communism, or anything. They just don't like the government. They join in a vague sort of way because an army colonel felt like raping a sister or a man's arm was cut off for trying to keep his only buffalo, and suddenly they are dangerous insurgents. But our village is pretty far from the centre of the fighting, in a region that is known to be a rebel stronghold. Most times the army doesn't have the stomach even to enter the area.

'Pa was middle-level rebel hierarchy, heading a little rebel unit. It seems he had an argument with someone at an area meeting. He came home drunk that night, and a while later the man he had an argument with came along, and he was drunk as well. He went up to my father who was sitting outside the house, announced that an apology would not be enough and shot him three times in the head.

'We watched it happened so many times, Milton and I. A debt, an insult, little things like that. Sometimes they would bring in the bodies of the men who had been killed in the fighting. Then they would start to sing out their lives, because the spirit can carry messages to our ancestors. We ran away then, and somehow we always ran to the same place. There is a little hillock on the edge of the village, round and smooth, like the head of a bald man. It falls away on the far side, down to the endless plains. It reminded us of the head of Akimbo, one of the village elders, so we called it Akimbo's Head.

'We would run there trembling, away from what we had seen, away from the singing. Then we would cry as loud as we could to drown out the singing. We cried for what we had seen, they sang for what we could not.

Milton would hug me tight and point out over the distant, peaceful savannah to something, anything. Then we would hurl pebbles out over the grassland to shake the fear and confusion out of our bodies and tell each other that death would go away one day soon.'

Nestor fell silent. Then he went slowly over to a steel trunk in the corner of his room and rummaged about among the helicopters and the crumpled clothes. Pulling out a shabby-looking folder, he drew out a grimy envelope from it. He closed the steel trunk and sat down heavily on it, gazing at the tattered paper in his hand.

'It never did,' he said slowly.

'Well, you still have two more years to go,' said Philomena. Then she smiled. 'And it seems that if you judge things well that can be extended to six – three chances for each year is the formula, isn't it? And if it goes wrong you can marry me.'

Nestor looked up, startled. 'Don't worry!' Philomena said, laughing. 'It doesn't mean we have to be together, but at least you won't have to go back.'

Nestor's eyes drifted out of the window to where the dragonflies whirled around the forlorn street lamp. 'It is not so simple. Even sad homes can cash in little debts of happiness and call you back. And we always go.'

Sitting on the trunk, letter in hand, he seemed remote and alone. Philomena went over to him and held him in her arms, and if you had to put a time and date to it, it was the moment in her life that brought her closest to caring for someone without expectation of return.

'Do you feel no debt to this place, to your home?' asked Nestor.

97

Philomena sighed. 'I don't really know – it has never been tested. I have memories, though. Darkness and voices to start with. The flash of fireworks through a wrought-iron grill. A splash of silver in an evening sky. Things like that. Sounds, smells, sight. At first, the lack of it.' She hesitated, considering whether to tell Nestor about her blindness. 'Water under the bridge,' she said firmly. 'Seeing is feeling. Experiencing is feeling. What remains afterwards is most often only sentimental embellishment. I've never really dwelt upon *happiness* as such, or whether I am happy here.' She sighed. 'But I suppose I will always have debts to pay here.'

He had hoped she would realise that he was vulnerable then, that he needed someone to talk to, to love. But he dared not say it. Philomena would recoil, and even the love he had seen for a moment would be pushed away by such honesty.

They sat in silence till Philomena finally said, 'I should be off now.'

Nestor wanted desperately for her to stay with him. 'I'll walk with you to the station,' he said dully, and it hurt.

On the way Philomena bought some peanuts, simultaneously lecturing the vendor on how to treat his pet mongrel's sore knee. She kissed Nestor swiftly with her mouth full of peanuts and walked briskly away down the platform. Nestor watched her receding down the platform and realised that he was in love with this girl and there was nothing he could do to make her love him back. He believed she felt the same, but love's unexpressed needs remain only belief.

# Fourteen

'A *taxi*? Are you completely mad, or what?' screeched Nestor, his voice ascending to an incredulous falsetto.

Philomena had strolled into the Pride of Asia to meet Nestor, only to find him in the middle of an animated conversation with Kailash and Shakeel, and a boy she had not seen before whom they addressed as Vaman.

She dragged a chair over to the table and was descending into it when Kailash turned to her and said icily, 'Madam, a meeting is in progress. Kindly take a seat elsewhere till we have finished.'

Frozen in mid-descent, Philomena gaped at Kailash for a moment, then smiled apologetically and slipped into a chair on the next table.

'Now see here, Nestor,' continued Kailash smoothly. 'In business, the key words are movement, flexibility, diversification. We have to move quickly into new fields before the competition moves in. And let's face it, the helicopter division is not what it used to be. Profits are down, inventory is high. I am not saying it is your fault. The quality of the product is the problem. Soon you will have to keep shifting location every day to avoid yesterday's buyers, because you have no after-sales service facilities. I have suffered some setbacks myself at my usual points, but I'm lucky enough to have plenty of alternatives available and very little equipment to relocate. It is the same for Vaman. Also, his product is high quality. Okay, people do feel sorry for cripples, but what precision he has brought to folding his forearm into his shirt-sleeve! Even fooled that foul-mouthed bastard Constable Tikekar for a whole week! Why, only yesterday he managed to extract a whole rupee from the *sethia* who owns the cloth shop at Gowalia Tank. *One rupee!* From a man who counts the nails in his furniture every night before closing shop!' He nodded appreciatively. A fine product! Now Shakeel... well, we will have to review the cinema ticket black market. It is a dying industry.

'Now, as you know, Guptaji has been a sort of godfather to me and his brother has decided to give up driving his taxi. He has decided to hire somebody to drive the taxi, and I have decided that the person he is going to hire is you. It is literally falling into your lap, a regular cash cow! And all you can do is wail like a pregnant woman!'

'But I don't know how to drive!' Nestor protested. 'I only have a driving licence because the army back home was distributing them to anyone who was over fifteen as an incentive during some election. And anyway, it's not

100

valid in India.' Nestor sat back smugly, pleased with the insurmountable obstacles he had strewn in the way of Kailash's diversification plans.

Kailash gazed evenly at Nestor. 'Guptaji informs me that proper licensed drivers cost far too much to employ. So he will obtain a licence for you, my friend – no test, no formalities.' He leaned over and patted Nestor's cheek encouragingly. 'Every day you will be walking away with more money than you make in a month of selling helicopters! So tomorrow Guptaji's brother will deliver the cab to Pinto's garage for a touch-up. I have decided that some investment has to be made to make it more... attractive – it pays in the long run. Day after, we pick the car up from Pinto and you can start driving.'

'But I can't just start driving!' whined Nestor.

'No problem,' said Kailash. 'Shakeel will teach you.'

Nestor eyed Shakeel doubtfully. 'Does *he* know how to drive?'

'Well...' started Shakeel hesitantly. 'I worked for a bus company for a while – one of those companies that run coaches between Bombay and Goa.'

Nestor seemed reassured.

'As a cleaner,' continued Shakeel, 'but I know how to drive. I even drove the buses sometimes, when the driver would let me. I never had any problem, except running over a stray goat once. None of the passengers realised because it just felt like another bump on the road. Besides, they were too busy smoking hashish and hugging each other in universal love to notice.'

Nestor looked at Philomena miserably.

'Now,' said Kailash briskly. 'I will personally attend to doing up the cab, making it look really good. We will bring it to...'

'My house,' called out Philomena firmly from the next table. 'Nestor will be at my place. Bring it there.'

Kailash turned around, peeved by the interjection. Then, not finding the issue worthy of debate, he turned back and asked: 'Anything else? No? Good. Adjourned.' He stood up and walked out of the café, calling over his shoulder for someone to settle his bill.

Vaman and Shakeel trickled out as well, leaving Philomena grinning mischievously at Nestor's misery. 'I could teach you to drive too, you know,' she said. 'Except it'll be much more fun if Mr Shakeel does it – for me, that is,' she added, bursting out laughing.

And so it was that on a bright morning in Bandra, Sawant found himself urgently leaping out of the way of a Bombay taxi that had got it into its crazed mind to career wildly up the driveway of the Casa de Familia DaCruz. Sawant had reluctantly admitted to himself later that he had had adequate prior notice of its impending arrival – he had heard the distinctive splutter of a Bombay taxi many minutes before it actually made its homicidal entry through the gate near which Sawant had been serenely weeding a flower bed. The problem had arisen from his inability to distinguish the sound of the average Bombay taxi from the screaming ascent of the aeroplanes that climbed up into the air from the nearby Santa Cruz airfield. Sawant had presumed he was again being subjected to the marvels of flight.

As he sat in the dirt muttering darkly, the taxi made its manic way up the driveway, threatening all the time to disintegrate spontaneously. Alerted by the racket, the inhabitants of the Casa de Familia DaCruz gathered on the veranda to watch the performance. On no face was the horror more vivid than Nestor's.

Kailash hopped merrily out of the car. 'Well,' he said, waving his arm at the monster, 'what do you think?'

In order to express an opinion it is necessary to talk, and there did not seem to be anyone immediately capable. They watched a cursing Shakeel attempting to re-attach what looked like the gear lever to the steering shaft.

Philomena recovered. She pointed limply at Shakeel. 'What is he doing?'

As if on cue, Shakeel alighted from the cab, gear lever in hand. 'It keeps falling off,' he said, scratching his head and looking genuinely perplexed. 'The treads are a little worn, so you have to push it in firmly and hold it in when you want to change gears. I solved the problem by just putting it in second and leaving it there. A small problem,' he said dismissively. 'We will sort it out.'

Nestor groaned. Philomena, obviously made of sterner stuff, had by this time commenced a full inspection of the taxi and noticed what looked like a message pasted across the rear windshield in fluorescent lettering. She walked around to read it and stopped dead.

Noticing her expression, Kailash strutted over, gazing at the windshield proudly. 'Good, huh? My idea. Makes it more trendy.'

Emblazoned in bright orange and pink and green across the top of the windshield in a stylised running hand was the name *Romeo*. A little lower, across the centre, was the legend 'CAME ON BABY'.

'Isn't there something wrong there?' she whispered feebly.

'Why?' asked Kailash.

'Came on baby, huh?'

'Oh *haah*, *haah*. That's the problem, is it? Pinto told me he had made some changes for the sticker,' said Kailash in a dismissive tone. 'But he says it means the same thing.'

Philomena continued to gape at the alarming confession.

'Right,' said Kailash, rubbing his palms together briskly and turning towards Nestor. 'Ready for your first lesson?'

Nestor whimpered pathetically. His face contorted as he held his arm up before his face, like a vampire confronted with the holy cross. 'I'm not going anywhere near that thing!' he howled.

'Don't be such a baby!' said Philomena, smiling brightly. 'Kailash has put in a lot of work for you.'

'It isn't safe!' Nestor whinnied.

'There's nothing safe about driving a taxi in Bombay anyway,' said Kailash.

'Right, let me give it a shot,' said Philomena slapping Shakeel's shoulder and taking the gear lever from his hand.

Tehmina suddenly leapt forward screeching. 'Over my dead body!'

Nestor charged across to restrain Philomena, and was neatly pushed by Shakeel and pulled by Philomena into

the driving seat. Doors shuddered shut and Nestor was
on his way to becoming Romeo, who, legend had it, had
come on baby.

# *Fifteen*

About the time Nestor was receiving his driving lesson from Shakeel, Edson DaCruz was slowly mounting the grand steps of the Western Railway headquarters at Churchgate.

The way people carry themselves is always telling, and Edson's manner was tired and hunched, perhaps a little defeated. He had begun to stoop a little, and his wrinkles had grown sad edges. The business had not been going well lately and the losses haunted his manner and appearance. After the departure of the British, the slide had been swift and crushing. The railways had continued to expand, but in a way that was slipping out of the reach of Edson's comprehension. At first the new Indian officers all knew him and appreciated that the favours granted to him had been based on the integrity of his work as much as his ability to discuss Mendelssohn with the *firangis*. But now the whole structure of influence and largesse was redefining itself, starting to settle and descend to the bottom of the barrel like muck does in water, and Edson was being left suspended and rudderless somewhere above. Strings were pulled in Delhi and puppets danced all over the government offices in free India as middlemen, power brokers and wheeler-dealers slowly strangled and crushed the old, friendly system.

The noose tightened relentlessly around the fortunes of 'Timotio & Son, Purveyors of Fine Timber'. Contract after contract slipped through Edson's fingers: 'I would like to help you Mr DaCruz, but...'; 'Instructions are awaited...'; 'I'm sorry Mr DaCruz, it is not in my hands...' The decisions were coming from people who Edson did not understand and places he could not have imagined being in. Bit by bit, the officers at headquarters in Bombay were by their complicity chipping away at their own authority.

Edson sat in the anteroom of G D Malik, Chief Superintendent (Procurement), Western Railway. Somewhere in the rafters far above him a fan grated rhythmically. Edson sat perched on the visitors' sofa, knees together, running his fingers nervously over the frayed rim of the *sola topi* resting on his lap. He gazed down idly at it. 'Dean's, 18 Rampart Row, Bombay, India' said the label on the inside. He sighed quietly. Dear, gentle old Arthur Dean. Faced with dwindling custom and a rapacious new landlord, he had packed his things and sorrowfully closed his doors forever. When was it, now? It had been soon after the coronation of the queen and Hunt's success on Everest (for Edson it was always Hunt – Hillary and Tenzing were only logistical coincidences). The new *sola topi* would have to be ordered, the material procured from far away. The days when Edson would not have thought twice about the expense had slipped away with Mr Dean. The crisp white shirts he bought from The Great Western Store were still starched crisp, but the brilliant white had mellowed with age, and his suspenders were frayed where the metal clasps bit into the cloth.

Edson had sat down one evening in his study at the Casa de Familia DaCruz and methodically drawn up a list of priorities. Top of the list was the payment of the property taxes for the house and trying to maintain it in good repair. Even there he was slowly losing the battle. Sawant wasn't getting all the manure he needed, so parts of the garden had had to be abandoned to the bramble, and if you went round to the rear of the house or even into the more remote rooms inside you could plainly see the peeling fortunes of Edson DaCruz hanging from the walls. The roof had plastic sheets drawn over cracked or broken tiles to keep the rain and insects out. On stormy nights the wind would sometimes blow the sheets away and the heavens would weep over the crumbling innards of the Casa de Familia DaCruz. A new *sola topi* did not feature on the list at all.

A buzzer exploded violently above the door to the superintendent's room. The PA rose from his battered desk and disappeared through the door. Edson patted down his hair and adjusted his tie to hide the stain under the collar button. The PA returned and disinterestedly gestured to Edson that he should go in.

Edson stood up and shuffled nervously towards the door, clutching the *sola topi* in front of him with both hands. Suddenly remembering, he straightened his hunch as he went into Malik's office.

Malik looked up and smiled broadly. 'Hull-lo, Hull-lo, DaCruz *Saab*! Take a seat, take a seat.'

Edson mumbled a thank you and sat down opposite Malik.

'Hah, so,' said Malik, picking up some papers. 'I have seen your proposal. But you know DaCruz *Saab*, the Mankurd-Bhiwandi line is a very big project.'

Edson nodded respectfully, thinking to himself that in the old days it would have just been another of many. Today, if he lost the order he would almost certainly have to shut down.

'And you know,' continued Malik, 'anything major goes to the Railway Board in Delhi. Approvals come from there, also suggestions on appointments, awarding contracts, and so on. Of course, they only call them "recommendations", but we all know what they mean. Now look at this,' he said, pointing at a piece of paper on the desk. 'Arrived yesterday from Delhi. All major materials contracts for projects are to be awarded only after floating a tender.'

Edson nodded dumbly. A tender was a concept which he had only a hazy awareness of. A tender meant that things were getting beyond him.

'So we will be floating a tender soon for the sleepers too.' Malik saw the panic in Edson's eyes. 'Don't worry. I cannot forget your kindness in the times when you need not have looked twice at us. I will call you the minute things start moving.'

'Thank you, sir,' said Edson. 'Only one question...'

'Sure, sure. What?'

'Who decides which tender to accept?'

'See, a committee will be set up. I will also be on it, but you know there can never be any guarantees when there is a committee. It is vital to submit your tender properly. How it is presented, what it says, what it avoids saying, how to leave room for manoeuvre. And you know Edson *Saab*, these days it has all become big business – who speaks to whom, who gets to the right places. This is all off the record of course, but for submitting the tender I suggest that you take Divakar's help. He has understood the system. He can point you in the right direction.'

'But sir,' protested Edson, looking perplexed, 'he is only a junior supervisor! And if the decision doesn't even rest with you, how can *he* be important?'

Malik leaned back and tilted his chair over till it rested against the wall behind him. Leaning over the side, he spat out a huge gob of *paan* into the rubbish bin. Then he fished out a packet of Wills Navy Cuts from his trouser and proceeded to light one, gazing steadily at Edson all the time. Shaking out the match, he said, 'I am sorry to say this, Edson *Saab*, but you must have noticed by now that the issue is not who is *entitled* to decide but who *actually* decides. Divakar has their ear. Go to him.'

Malik smiled at Edson's confusion. 'Yes I know,' he said, throwing his head back and staring reflectively into the recesses of the ceiling. 'I know that Divakar is still only a supervisor because in the old days someone complained that he had asked for a bribe.' He looked down sharply at Edson again. 'You.' He rocked forward and waved his hand dismissively. 'Don't worry. He will not hold it against you. He is a businessman. Meet him. He is more important than I am.'

Edson thought he detected a flash of regret in the superintendent's voice. He wearily stood up to leave.

As he reached the door Malik called out to him: 'Edson *Saab*! If there is anyone left among us today who is entitled to walk with his head held high it is you. So why do you walk as if your back is broken?'

Edson closed the door behind him and crossed the antechamber to the PA's desk. The PA pushed a piece of paper across to him without looking up from his papers. 'You will find him there. Tell him that Malik will be speaking to him.'

*

Edson crossed Queens Road to the terminus. As he shuffled across the concourse towards the first-class ticket window a group of lounging students turned to look at him, smiling quietly at his attire. He looked up as he reached the window, hesitated a moment, and moved away and joined the queue for second-class tickets.

Seated behind the iron bars on the window of the train home, Edson thought back to how he had followed the directions on the slip given to him by the PA. Of how he had found Milind Divakar chatting at his neighbour's table in the huge common well on the third floor of the office. Divakar's eyes had narrowed momentarily when he saw Edson. He had greeted him a shade too heartily,

111

asking him how he could help 'the great Sir Edson'. Edson told him about the tender. 'Sure, sure, lovely,' Divakar had said, moving towards his own desk. 'The Bhiwandi project, I suppose. But it is not possible to do anything here,' he said, casting a conspiratorial glance around the office. 'Anyway, a member of the Railway Board is in Bombay today and I have to meet him this evening. Why don't we meet at the Imperial tomorrow? About seven in the evening? Fine.' Divakar had pulled out a diary from his shirt pocket and drawn out a shiny, expensive Parker from a drawer with great deliberation. After making the entry in his diary he had leaned back in his chair, pointedly caressing the pen. 'Nice, no? A kind gift from a grateful contact,' he had said, smiling slyly.

Edson watched the stations roll by: Churchgate, from where he had boarded the train, Marine Lines, Charni Road, Grant Road, Bombay Central. He thought it funny that so many stations should go by without an Indian name appearing. Big project! Huh! Just up-and-down stuff in the old days. Now, if it didn't come through it would probably mean the end of the business. Timotio & Son had never operated on credit and Edson wasn't going to be the one to start. If he couldn't pay his bills on his own and promptly, he would simply close.

He thought back on his life. Lancelot, safely settled at university in Leeds, making steady and unspectacular progress and eating great big holes in the dwindling resources of the DaCruzes. Philomena, the wayward apple of his eye, stalking every rule with a view to a kill. How was he going to support all this and the house too if he lost out on this tender? He sighed. Fifty-nine is not an age to reach the crossroads of your life, he thought to himself.

Three coaches further up the same train, Philomena was lounging in the empty first-class compartment re-reading *Brave New World* between bouts of daydreaming about the driving lesson.

As the train pulled into the ancient arches of Bandra station she slid off the train before it came to halt and slipped out through the exit before Edson had even alighted from the train. She had telephoned ahead from the hostel for the car and was already on her way home when Edson emerged from the station.

Edson walked across the station square ramrod-straight, his head held at an angle of authority and importance, nodding imperiously at acquaintances and familiar local faces as he briskly hailed a taxi.

# Sixteen

Now one must not be prejudiced by the fact that when Nestor suddenly jammed his foot on Romeo's brake pedal at the bottom of the hill at Mount Mary the back door flew open and batted Mrs Saldanha's ample bottom as she stood buying a candle from a Novena stall on the pavement. Nor should one be put off by the fact that in a moment of abject terror Nestor managed to break the detachable gear lever in half, thus converting the gear-changing process into a sort of cooperative effort: Shakeel would at the appropriate moment shove the truncated stump into its socket and howl to Nestor to 'press the pedal'. It is not even important that Kailash, who was holding on to the bottom-smacking door, almost lost his fingers to a wall that was rearranging Romeo's paintwork. And it probably didn't affect Romeo's oil sump as much as Pinto at the garage made out when Nestor took a somewhat unnecessary detour over the road-divider at Mahim. Certainly Kailash did not think that anything unusual had happened, steadfastly providing solid encouragement to Nestor all through.

The simple fact was that Nestor was both a quick learner as well as something of a natural when it came to driving. His understanding of the dynamics of acceleration and braking was adequate within the first few minutes. His judgement of distances improved vastly within the hour, and by the time they were winding down the lesson, his instinct for gear changes was vastly superior to Shakeel's, though modesty stopped him from overriding Shakeel's instructions. Within the week Nestor was the undisputed Romeo of the road and Shakeel had been banished to the rear seat, from where he looked upon his protégé with fond pride. Kailash remained unmoved and businesslike, never having had any doubts about the enterprise in the first place.

The next day, Divakar telephoned Edson and suggested that they meet at the entrance to the hotel. At seven minutes to seven Edson stood outside the entrance to the Imperial hotel at Ballard Pier nervously tucking in his shirt to hide the bit where it had caught in a door handle, torn, and been darned. He was wearing his finest bow tie, his shoes brightly polished: if he was going to be seen with the grasping scoundrel he was at least going to make sure that it looked as though it was he who was in charge.

Divakar kept Edson waiting on the pavement till well past half past seven. When he eventually arrived he greeted Edson without apology and strode into the hotel with the air of a man in familiar but hostile territory, like a low-bred millionaire at a tea party for the titled. The waiters nodded at him with polite coldness. Sitting down, he snapped his fingers twice at a waiter and ignoring the menu proffered, reeled off his requirements.

'Bring me a plate of chicken *malai tikka*, one *shammi kabab*, one *pahadi kabab*, two large Scotches, soda, a *Kalkatta meetha paan* and a packet of State Express – and bring some *masala papads* and peanuts also.' Divakar waved in Edson's direction. 'Ask him what he wants.'

Edson asked for a small rum and soda. And a stirrer.

As the waiter walked away, Divakar leaned back and gazed with malevolent amusement at Edson, scratching his groin contemplatively. 'So you see, Mr Edson,' he said in a thick, self-satisfied voice, 'in the end we are all the same.' He sniggered quietly to himself, gazing at Edson.

'Now let's see...,' he said, snapping out of his little gloat. 'Ghanshyamdas & Sons, Jai Constructions and West Coast Timber are all in the race. And you. Ghanshyamdas is banking on Polly Patel, the Member of Parliament from Rajkot to speak to the correct people on the Railway Board. Jai...' he trailed off, lapsing into thought. 'Jai are crooks. They meet you, take your advice, then haggle with you when you ask for your fees. But they are dangerous because their cousin works in the PMO.'

Edson looked puzzled. 'PMO?'

Divakar let out a despairing sigh. 'Prime Minister's Office,' he said slowly and deliberately, as if explaining to an imbecile. Then he turned sharply to the waiter, who was pouring soda into Divakar's drink. 'Stop, you bleddy fool! If I want plain soda I can ask, no? Where are my cigarettes?'

Divakar took a long, luxurious slurp at his whisky and continued. 'West Coast are using Jiggs Jhangiani and Bubbly Singh. They are both well-respected ex-IAS men, but they don't have much clout. I don't think West Coast has a chance,' he concluded.

'And you,' he said, pointing at Edson and smiling, 'are using me.' He made the statement as though he had just laid down the ace of trumps. He let out a little giggle and then burst into laughter, shaking his head from side to side. He wiped the tears of mirth from his eyes with a napkin, still shaking his head. 'What a day! What a day!' He regarded Edson with an amused look. Edson smiled uncertainly and looked down at the table, focusing on a *paan*-red droplet on the lip of Divakar's whisky glass.

'There are a few others,' continued Divakar. 'But they are all small-timers. Useless *lakdawalas*! We will be rejecting them out of hand. As soon as the tender forms are out I want you to send me a letter signed by you saying that you are tendering for the contract as per the attached form. The form I will fill in myself. Then of course there is the matter of contacting people, speaking to them, convincing them. There will be expenses, so send me an advance... say, a thousand rupees. After the tender has been submitted we will settle the accounts, but a thousand I will need by say... Friday?' Edson said nothing. 'Good,' said Divakar, picking up the last of the kebabs. Then he put it down again and pushed the plate towards Edson. Edson politely declined the offer.

Divakar popped the *kabab* into his mouth and leaned back in his chair, gazing at Edson thoughtfully. Abruptly, he threw out his arms and exclaimed: 'Why are you worried? When I take on a job I do it professionally. I'm a businessman, you see. I don't care if you think I am the worst *hijra* bastard in the world. I will still do your work honestly so long as you pay me for it. And if you want to work in the new India, you will now have to work with people like me.' He smiled comfortingly, as if to suggest that the prospect wasn't that bad.

The waiter arrived and handed the bill to Edson without needing any prompting. Divakar drained what was left of the whisky, which the *paan* had by now had turned a turbid pink. 'Good,' he repeated. 'Now let us go.'

At the entrance Divakar patted his pockets. 'Oh, I've forgotten my purse at the office. Could you lend me a hundred rupees to go home? You see, I have gout and at this time of the night I usually go home by taxi. Fully adjustable, okay?'

He clambered into a taxi and without bothering that Edson could hear him, instructed the driver to take him to Suzie Rani, a brothel on Foras Road that even Edson had heard of.

Edson stood on the pavement and counted his money. It was just enough to either take a taxi to Churchgate or a taxi home from Bandra station. He decided that it would be more pleasant to walk home from the station along the sea.

His eyes stinging with anger, he walked home along Carter Road that night trying to ignore the sorrowing

118

street lamps and the tender sighs of the moonlit sea. He was haunted by Divakar's gloating face, his own helplessness, the conspiracy of history. He found he had been grinding his train ticket to a pulp as he walked, and flung it to the pavement in anger. After a few steps he stopped and turned back, looking around in the dark for the ball of paper. Picking it up, he slipped it into his trouser pocket and continued on home, shoulders hunched. There was no one on the road to keep up appearances for.

# Seventeen

Kailash had as usual been right about the taxi business. Romeo was the syndicate's cash cow, and there was a little extra money to spend now. A steady stream of *ice-golas* and *vada-paos* bore tasty testimony to the success of Nestor's exertions at the wheel. Nestor and Philomena saw less and less of each other. The more he worked the more money he made, and late-night fares were always more rewarding.

The absences were a blessing, for when they did meet they went to each other with renewed frenzy. They stole away to the deserted road behind the navy barracks at Colaba and made love in Romeo. They took long rides to Marve Beach, where the rich had places to relax and the rest scraped around to find quiet places to neck.

Slowly, inevitably, they began to be comfortable with each other. The tingle in the other's touch began to recede, like a ripple on still water disturbed, till there were no ripples at all. They began to invite Kailash and the others along on their outings, and Kailash took over as the focus of their meetings instead of their own togetherness. His stories, often fuelled by Philomena's inexhaustible supply of hash, were magical.

Late one evening at Manori beach Kailash was cheerily performing cartwheels in the sand while simultaneously attempting to whistle a tune from *Haathi Mere Saathi*, a smash-hit Hindi film. Philomena looked on in amusement.

'So what do your parents have to say about you?' asked Philomena.

Kailash started another cartwheel, pondering the question. He stopped halfway through, balanced on his hands for moment, then grounded his feet. Standing up, he threw his arms outwards. 'It is only half a problem. My father died when I was three. Cut to pieces by a Virar Fast while crossing the railway tracks,' he said, making vigorous scything motions for emphasis. 'It seems he was rushing across, late for work.'

Kailash resumed his assault on *Haathi Mere Saathi* and walked over to where Philomena was sitting. 'It just struck me,' he said, flopping down beside her. 'What a terrible mistake to make! Dying is not such a good idea anyway, but imagine dying because you are late for work! Obviously a hopeless sort of fellow!' He spent a few moments swirling the sand around with his hands. 'My mother is all right. She has three different jobs – first she sweeps and swabs floors at two places on Malabar Hill, then she walks all the way to Tardeo in the afternoon to wash clothes and dishes there. And all for what? Sixty-five rupees! When I tell her that I can support her she cuffs me on the head! I tried to give her some money once, told her that I had become an entrepreneur. I even bought her a new pair of *chappals* and she threw her old ones at me! But she kept the new ones all the same. She said I had become a thief! I ask you,' he said, looking injured, 'is this a parent's gratitude? So now I give her nothing. Every day after collecting water from the municipal tap at five in the morning, she bathes and makes a little lunch. Two-thirds to me, a third for herself. Every day I leave it behind. And in the evening I tell her that the ladies who run the technical training school she has enrolled me in gave us lunch and that I am not hungry, which is usually true. I can make out she doesn't believe me, but she says nothing and quietly finishes the food.'

'And when you *are* hungry?'

'I just curse myself for miscalculating.'

'Doesn't she wonder about it?'

'A long time ago, I bought myself a new pair of "Disco Floater" slippers. She demanded to know where I had got the money from. I refused to tell her. Now when I buy something and take it home she looks at me accusingly but doesn't ask questions any more. She pretends it does not bother her, but I can see the shame in her face and I think that one day she will die of it.'

He slapped his thighs in a gesture of finality. 'Well, it's not my problem,' he said softly.

'Oi, *bhaiya*!' Kailash suddenly bellowed to a passing vendor. 'Make me a *batata-puri*, and for once in your miserable life use the potatoes like you don't own them!'

Philomena asked whether he had any brothers or sisters.

'A sister. Dead before she was born. There was no time for any more before my father died.'

'Do you remember him at all, your father?' asked Philomena.

Kailash stopped swirling sand. 'A little bit here, a little bit there. I remember him trying to teach me how to bat, and once when he told me that he would make sure that I grew up to be more than he was.' Kailash smiled wryly, his eyes out over the sea. 'Well, I have certainly become a businessman earlier than expected!'

He looked across at Philomena and grinned broadly, the tears glinting in his eyes. Then he turned away quickly when he saw that Philomena had noticed. 'Come on, you slouch!' he shouted to the *bhel-puri* vendor. 'We haven't got all day! We are busy people, see?'

*

Among the various secluded spots that Nestor and Philomena found to pursue their passion was one just past the entrance to the Hanging Gardens, where Ridge Road drops down towards Kemp's Corner in a lazy arc. The sprawling old trees of the garden lined one side of the road, the thick forests of the Towers of Silence the other. Nestor would park Romeo halfway down this stretch a discreet distance from the little cigarette shop on the pavement. From time to time Philomena would glance over to the side entrance of the Towers of Silence on the other side of the road, imagining the horror that would lash the White Cassocks' faces if they saw her making love to a 'black boy'.

One day, Philomena stuck a finger up at a passing priest who was attempting to peer into Romeo. He scuttled away through the gates, more distressed by Philomena's state of undress than by her gesture, which he could not possibly have understood.

Some days later, as Nestor parked Romeo at the spot, two policemen appeared and peered officiously in through the windows.

'Why have you stopped? What is your business here? Obscene activities?' asked one.

'We have had complaints!' said the other.

'From the *bawaji* priests in there,' said the first, jerking a disrespectful thumb over his shoulder in the direction of the Towers. 'People are using this place for nefarious purposes. Come on, move on!'

'No, no sir,' said Philomena, the childlike innocence in her voice startling Nestor. 'I have to come here everyday. To meet the priest. He takes me to the Hanging Gardens for training thrice a week in the evening. He's teaching me to recite prayers from our holy book. He says my breath has to develop a little more before I can do it correctly, so he massages my chest every evening. I pay him fifty rupees a month for the lessons and we haven't even started reading from the book yet! Sometimes I think...' She let her voice trail off and blinked innocently, looking anxiously from one policeman to the other.

The policemen's eyes narrowed. 'Is that so?' said one of them tersely. 'And what does this priest look like?'

Philomena proceeded to provide the policemen with an accurate description of the priest she had intimidated with her nakedness a few days earlier.

'Well, I suggest that you stop wasting your money,' said one of the policemen, smiling grimly. 'Anyway, your teacher may not be free to give you lessons for a while.'

'Actually,' said Philomena earnestly, 'I was thinking of stopping anyway. Lately while massaging me he has been touching me more and more...' her voice trailed off again.

Nestor was alarmed at the brutal anticipation in the eyes of the policemen as they turned away and strode towards the gate across the road.

Somehow, when they returned to the spot some days later things had changed forever. Perhaps their exertions had run their course, or perhaps the enjoyment they had derived from the encounter with the policemen had brought home to them the monotony of their trysts. For whatever reason, the drive up past the Hanging Gardens had lost its magic. The thrill that had earlier run through them on the way up had been lost and the slow descent into habit had begun, with neither willing to force the issue for fear of causing hurt.

One evening at the end of Nestor's day shift, after the usual cup of tea at the usual Pride of Asia, they drove down the usual Marine Drive towards the usual Ridge Road, each silently grappling with the boredom that sat heavily with them in the car. As they approached the storm-warning signal at the end of Marine Drive Nestor casually asked, 'Do you want to go up?', as though it had become an option. Philomena shook her head silently.

As Nestor turned the car away from Ridge Road and up Babulnath he felt part-relieved and part-broken. They stopped for *kulfi* on the street corner back at Chowpatty, joking and slapping each other on the back like old friends. The texture of their relationship had shifted irrevocably. They had stepped back from the physical, and perhaps moved a little closer to love.

When Nestor dropped her at Grant Road station that night to catch the train home to Bandra she only touched him lightly on the shoulder and got out quickly.

'See you tomorrow,' she said through the window. 'Come any time after nine – nothing happens before then.'

As Nestor drove away he pondered over whether he should actually go to this infamous college social, this annual occasion well known to incorporate the sort of activities that the management of Jesuit or trust-operated colleges would consider to be a one-way ticket to the enduring flames of hell. Perhaps he would go. Then again, he probably would not know anyone there apart from a couple of Philomena's friends, who he knew only vaguely.

The next day Philomena was bright and insistent on the telephone. 'You are coming,' she said firmly. 'I'll be there early – there are a couple of things to organise. You can come when you finish for the day. Bye.' All in one breath in the space of ten seconds, with no room for manoeuvre. That was that, thought Nestor, smiling at the telephone.

# *Eighteen*

'Very fine, very fine!' said Narayan 'Kartoos' Kenkre, State Minister for Education and chief guest at the pre-mayhem segment of the social. 'Fine decorations!' He waved a podgy hand around the venerable old Cowasji Jehangir Hall, its glory enhanced by the efforts of the principal, Miss Cama, and Rebecca Saldanha, the chairman of the Students' Union. 'Really beautiful!' he exclaimed, casually leaning sideways to see if he could snatch a glimpse of Miss Cama's non-existent cleavage. 'Now,' he bellowed bluffly, 'where am I to sit?'

Kenkre had been nicknamed Kartoos the Bullet by the popular press, ostensibly for his ability as a political troubleshooter, but the real reason was his ability to live up to his nickname in the more sordid guest houses of Falkland Road. Rising to address the congregation, which was thin and as yet reverential, he delivered an excruciating sermon on the importance of social and extracurricular activities for young minds, stopping periodically to scratch his groin with obvious relish. He nodded at the polite applause at the end of his speech and pronounced that the proceedings were now 'in session'.

For the next hour Kenkre watched the dance floor, where a few students were dancing listlessly. They were the ones who had lost out in the draw that morning to determine who should entertain the authorities till they departed. Kenkre yawned as Miss Cama conducted a polite conversation with him, his eyes roving the hall. He leaned back over his shoulder towards his bodyguard and said something to him. The man crossed the hall towards a group of students dancing politely and spoke to one of the girls.

Kenkre leered appreciatively at Philomena as she sauntered along towards him behind the bodyguard.

'You are a very fine dancer,' he said. He pronounced dancer the American way. 'Now,' he said, his eyes savaging Philomena's breasts, 'perhaps we can have a dance also?' American accent still intact.

'Well, you see, sir,' said Philomena, thinking to herself that she was really getting to be rather good at this little-girl-lost voice, 'I have a boyfriend. He is a special boy, and if I dance with anyone else he gets very depressed. I only did it once before, and he tried to hang himself. I hope you will understand.'

Alarm bells rang violently in Kenkre's head. He could see the headlines: 'College Student Commits Suicide – Minister Kenkre Involved'.

'No matter, no matter,' said Kenkre resting a podgy

128

hand reassuringly on Philomena's hip. 'Perhaps we can meet for dinner sometime?'

'Certainly,' said Philomena very loudly. 'I would love to meet you for dinner. Perhaps with your family? I am told that Mrs Kenkre is an accomplished *Kathakali* dancer. It would be wonderful to meet her.'

Kenkre's face froze. 'Oh, yes, yes. I will ask my secretary to be in touch,' he said hastily, making a mental note to do nothing of the sort. He dismissed Philomena with a wave and turned his attentions elsewhere.

Kenkre was a fat, flabby man, totally unsuited to hunting women, a scavenger able to satisfy himself with whatever came his way with the minimum effort and the maximum return. One by one he ran through the girls present, propositioning them and smilingly accepting their monotonous refusals with mounting rage. Finally he gave up and sat sulkily in a corner next to Mrs Wadia of the Literature Department, who instantly proceeded to enlighten him about the peculiar problem she was facing. He was probably the only person present who had not yet heard of the sordid saga of the Oxford Student Union's dastardly efforts to hound her by sending an ambulance all the way to Bombay to spy on her, a situation she had endured since she had left Oxford in the summer of 1940. Kenkre, who was not listening, pondered the possibility of a quick detour to Tarabai's welcoming establishment on the way home. As he contemplated the mechanics of the endeavour something strange seemed to happen.

Most of the staff, with the tenacious exception of Miss Wadia, had left. It may have been his imagination, but the lights suddenly seemed to turn sultry, the movement of the bodies on the dance floor more languorous, the music more abrasive. Some primal wind had swept into the place, bringing with it dark forbidden edges full of smouldering expectations and restless friction. There was a tautness in the air which seemed to slide over and around the dancers. Kenkre noticed that the extra-smart girl in the short skirt who he had propositioned first was moving on her own in the dark, and despite his bitterness he admired the slow, lazy circle she made with her hips before she snapped them forward.

Philomena whirled and ground as the music seeped into her. Kenkre stared open-mouthed at this magnificent animal as it made love to the air, the music, itself. The sweat dripped off Kenkre's forehead as profusely as it did off Philomena's drenched and frenzied body. He watched as she grabbed hold of a boy and ground him into the dust. Discarding him, she devoured another, slaughtered a third. And still there was no respite. *Saali randi*, he thought to himself, where is this boyfriend of yours now? One by one, the girls who had rebuffed him swirled across his eyes as he trembled with impotent rage. He jerked out of his chair and stormed out of the room, intent upon a night of brutality and abuse with Tara or Tamiko or Priya or anyone else unfortunate enough to be free to endure his attentions.

Rudely jerked out of her lament, Miss Wadia watched open-mouthed as the minister strode out of the hall. She gathered up her things and scurried out herself, eyes darting about for lurking ambulances.

130

The morning after the social, Kenkre woke up and blew his nose. He wiped his hands on the bed sheet, and ordered a fresh set of sheets and sat down to consider the position. Something would have to be done. He was far too shrewd a politician to consider exacting his revenge upon that insolent whore who had lied to him. Gutter morals, he told himself. Quite capable of actually calling up the wife, and that would mean a career setback of perhaps insurmountable proportions. He set his jaw and grimly got down to work.

'Minister Castigates Social Activities' was the irresistible headline in the *Evening News of India* that same evening. 'Minister Refuses to Tango' was the choice of *Blitz*, under a large and uncomplimentary photograph of Kenkre. Even the venerable old *Times of India* carried several column inches on its front page under the dynamic heading 'College Social Draws Flak from Minister'. The statement issued by Kenkre was carried in its entirety by all: 'It is with regret that this government finds it necessary to impose a comprehensive ban on the annual college socials of all colleges funded or part-funded by the state government in view of the disgraceful and unbecoming behaviour of students of a city college at their recently-held function at the Cowasji Jehangir Hall, Bombay. The lack of discipline and manifestly improper and immoral behaviour exhibited at the function is inimical to the great culture and traditions of this city, the state of Maharashtra, our government, and the country. Government has therefore issued directions *vide* Circular Number 121/37/Ed/52-ARP-70 to all concerned institutions in this regard. Suitable notifications to this effect are being prepared and will be published in the State Gazette shortly.'

The editorial page of *The Workers' Herald*, under the wildly innovative headline 'Time to Ponder', proceeded to deliver a laborious treatise on the issue of '... the infiltration of contemporary global influences into the country and the consequential redefinition of indigenous youth culture and erosion of traditional values...', gloriously arriving at no conclusion whatsoever.

All the papers also carried Kenkre's second statement, read out by his secretary: 'I have never discouraged the extracurricular activities of students, who are the fruits and flowers of our great nation. Though I was informed prior to my attending the function that disco-style dancing was to take place, in disco there is no bodily contact. I am aware of all contemporary trends in dancing. The contact dancing I witnessed is called foxtrot. Boys and girls were touching each other. While these new dances may be acceptable in western countries, contacting is totally alien to our culture and traditions. The behaviour I witnessed was a disgrace to the college concerned and cannot be permitted by us. But more than that, we must all hang our heads in shame at their behaviour and strive to remove such behaviour from our social fabric.'

That was the exact text. While most newspapers carried the statement with suitable corrections, Minoo Masalawalla, the sprightly old editor of *Voice*, a tabloid at the lower and more entertaining end of the spectrum, carried the statement in its original form under the banner 'Disco Is Dandy: Kenkre'. Across the length and breadth of the city and its more fashionable clubs and restaurants the debate raged. Who had been involved? It was rumoured that Jeri Boyce, who had been present, had been whipped by her father and stripped of her share of the Boyce millions. Some of the boys who had been at the social were buttonholed in pivate by their fathers and a few of them, seeing a hint of admiration in their parents' eye, had been willing to confirm the rumours, even embellish them. The fathers in turn carried their sons' tales of bravado to the tennis courts and swimming pools of the city's clubs and gymkhanas. Even Edson, now reduced to a nervous wreck by the imminent opening of the tenders, vaguely asked Philomena if it was true and if she knew who they were talking about. Philomena had smiled at him and said that she didn't understand it and that perhaps they were talking about her. Edson had smiled at his daughter's humour and gone back to worrying.

Minoo Masalawala, all of eighty-five years at the time, wrote a long and dignified letter to various newspapers defending the students and stressing the futility of viewing the actions of youth with the weary hindsight of experience. He merrily proclaimed that it was common knowledge that in the last year he had slept with five happily married Bombay women without any damage being done to their standing at all. He condemned no one, but demanded that the same respect be shown to the students and concluded his letter with the observation that everyone's choices were entitled to respect.

The next day, the front page of the *Voice* carried an article written by Masalawala himself with the screaming headline 'Foxy Trotter!' below a large photograph of a shirtless Kartoos grinding his ample bosom against a half-naked lady who looked like someone who was doing her job. Beneath the photograph was the caption 'Kenkre the moral crusader takes a break from his convictions'. The photograph had obviously been taken through a window of the *Dhama Dham* Deluxe Guest House & Social Club, Forth Pasta Lane, a fact established by the signboard visible at the bottom of the photograph. The article pointed out that the owner of the hotel, Ms Tikki Khanna had, contrary to all rules, been given permission to open a discotheque in a residential building on Cuffe Parade. 'But then,' the article concluded, 'as we all know, the Honourable Minister has no objection to disco.'

Kenkre put down his morning cup of tea with shaking hands. The saucer rattled on the glass tabletop. He rushed away into his chamber and at the second attempt managed to dial the phone number correctly.

'Hello, sir,' he said in a wobbly voice. 'All lies! The photograph is bogus. And you know all about the *Voice*, all third-class people!' As he spoke his voice gathered indignation, comfortable with the mouthing of dishonesty.

'Oh, you haven't seen it today?' Kenkre calmed down, relieved. 'Sir,' he continued. 'I am going on tour for a few days to the district colleges. Talwalkar will attend the cabinet meeting this evening. Please excuse me.'

Replacing the receiver with relief he rushed away to get his things together. When he emerged again onto the veranda where he had been drinking his tea he saw his wife settling down to hers. 'I am going away on tour. I'll let you know where I am.'

134

'So suddenly?'

'It is an emergency,' he said, rushing to the waiting car.

As he got in, the telephone rang. His wife called out to him. 'The Chief Minister wants to speak to you.'

'Tell him I have left!' he howled.

'I can't. I have already told him that he is just in time.'

'Tell him you were wrong!' he shrieked.

His wife set the receiver down by the telephone. 'I have told you before, do not ever expect me to lie for you,' she said calmly, sitting down and picking up the newspapers from the table.

Kenkre groaned and made his way to the telephone. He picked up the receiver with trembling hands. 'Hello sir! Lucky,' he said in his most obsequious voice. 'I was just about to... but, sir... all lies... but if they are lies how can it matter to us?... yes, sir... yes, sir... thank you, sir.' Kenkre sank heavily onto the stool by the telephone. He saw his wife looking at him evenly, the *Voice* in her hand.

'Any more lies to be exposed, Mr Minister?' she asked quietly.

'Shut up, you old hag!' snarled Kenkre. 'I am not Minister any more.'

Those were the 'good old days' that people talk about today – the days when ministers actually resigned, or were instructed to.

*

You would have thought that the uproar that her actions had led to would have been the high point in Philomena's life at the time. But on that fateful night something far more important had happened.

135

Philomena had tried to nurse Nestor through that evening. He had been quiet and uncertain in the company of Philomena's friends. They had been polite enough, but unwilling to exchange more than pleasantries and platitudes with him. Philomena, who knew of the richness of his reading and the depth of his understanding, was irritated by his refusal to impose himself upon the conversation. She drank steadily from the cache of liquor stashed high in the galleries of the hall. The more she drank the more resentful she got, the more restricted by his presence she felt. She sought relief in the abandonment of dance, but Nestor retreated in confusion and pain after she passionately bit into his chest. Her dancing became more and more abandoned, and he could see the unfocused, indiscriminate passion in her glazed eyes. He walked quickly out of the hall in disgust.

Leaning against his cab and gazing vacantly at the lights of the Regal Cinema Circle, Nestor did not know it then, but he was quietly redefining his approach to Philomena forever. He stood there a long while, believing he was thinking of nothing in particular. Finally, he decided to go in again and was surprised at how calm and assured he felt. As he made to go, Philomena came out with one of the boys he had been introduced to. They were holding onto each other, and he could see her nails digging into his waist and the lust glinting in her eyes. He stopped and watched as they entered a parked car. He saw their silhouettes merge, and then the boy's shadow disappeared downwards into Philomena's lap and her head snapped back. He felt calm, detached. He was surprised at how easily he could ignore the hurt. The boy's head reappeared. The car started, and Philomena was gone.

Nestor slowly got into the cab, a wry smile on his face. As he drove away, he felt strangely superior.

# Nineteen

'I think we should remember that nobody owns anybody. I am not beholden to you for anything, and you are not to me.' Philomena was sitting cross-legged on the old cane chair at the far end of the veranda at the Casa de Familia DaCruz. Nestor leaned casually on the railing, looking disinterested.

'Did you really want to leave with that fellow? I mean, I don't really care what you did with him, but did you really want to do it with him?' Nestor asked casually.

'No, but I thought you had left and I had to get home somehow, didn't I? Besides, it was quite good.'

'You didn't seem to be in any condition to be able to remember that,' he said dryly.

'You'd be surprised,' she said brutally. 'You know the problem? The problem is not that you really care any more, or that you feel betrayed. It's just a question of the loss of possession, of control. That is what you cannot handle.'

Nestor shrugged his shoulders. 'I'll live,' he said, sounding bored. 'So what's all this about that fat bastard Kenkre?'

Philomena smiled. 'Didn't like going away empty-handed, so to speak. He even propositioned me.'

'He can obviously tell which women are likely to be available,' said Nestor.

Philomena felt a rush of anger. She bit her lip and said nothing.

After a long silence, Philomena unwound herself in the chair and got up with a sigh. 'Fuck this,' she said, walking off towards the door that led into the house. Nestor followed in her wake, intending to depart the other way himself.

As he reached the steps, Edson was climbing up to the veranda. He looked old, diminished. Ignoring Nestor's greeting, he sank wearily into an armchair on the veranda and stared out vacantly over the advancing tangleweed in the garden, picking at the frayed ends of the upholstery.

Are you all right, sir?' asked Nestor.

Edson seemed to take an age to train his haunted eyes on Nestor. 'Would you sell,' he said, very slowly, 'all the music in your life for a polite letter? All of it – your Lippatti, your Kreisler, the Arrau box set you even put back painting the house for? Gigli, Britten, Oistrach, Hask... You cried and laughed with them. Talked to them. Rejoiced with them. Fell in and out of love to them. Drank to them.' He fell silent. He held out the envelope in his hand.

Philomena, whose departure had been arrested by Edson's outpouring, snatched the letter and read it impatiently, as if was an unnecessary intrusion. She handed it back huffily to Edson. 'For God's sake! It's just another contract! Not getting it isn't the end of the world. There is more to life, you know.' Philomena swept off into the house.

Nestor hesitated. He felt sorry for Edson. Unlike Philomena, he had absorbed what Edson had just said and was saddened that something had been able to part Edson and his music. Unable to find anything useful to say, he muttered his apologies and started down the steps to the garden.

As he walked away Edson shouted after him. 'Never surrender your own happiness to the world – it is too stupid and shallow to understand the sacrifice!'

Nestor turned and saw Edson staring into the distance, clutching the letter in his fist and still pulling sadly on the tattered strands of upholstery.

As he gazed unseeing at the jumble of undergrowth and neglect creeping towards the steps of the Casa de Familia DaCruz, Edson wondered where all the order had gone from his life. Was the lost key hiding somewhere in this maze of applications and tenders and influence and deceit? Why did he not know where to look? Why could he not understand how to find it again? Was it there at all, or had it left with the foreigners who he had understood better than his own people?

Tehmina came out onto the veranda. Without a word he handed her the letter. She sat down next to Edson and read it. After a while, she patted his hand gently. 'Don't worry so much. We won't starve. If it comes to it, we can always sell this place,' she said, gesturing around with her hand.

140

Edson turned to her, the desolation plain in his eyes. 'Can't you see? I am already starving! I am starved of everything, everyone. The work I knew, the people I knew... I even have to lie! They wanted me to host the bridge dinner at the gymkhana. What was I to do? Tell them I couldn't afford to?' He looked down into his lap. 'I told them I was doing a big new project, that I would not have the time.'

*

Nestor's cultivated indifference reaped its whirlwind. Irked by the loss of power, the prising away of her hold over him, Philomena's attempts to provoke Nestor became increasingly extreme, and the more outrageous they became the less they seemed to affect Nestor. The grim downward spiral continued, destructive of everything positive in their relationship, brutalised by weakness and pride. The sex got better the further apart they were driven, stoked by the same pride and distance that was destroying another part of them.

*

'I will always be with you, my dear. Wherever in this world you choose to go.' Tehmina gently stroked Edson's stubble, her eyes resting soft and sorry upon him. They were lying side by side in Edson's bedroom, gazing up at the crumbling roof above them.

A letter had arrived from Eustace, a cousin of Edson's who had disappeared into the world a long time ago. He had resurfaced in Hong Kong, running what seemed to be a flourishing business trading in paper. The global family newswires had been busy. Eustace knew all about the hard times Edson had fallen upon. The letter offered Edson a solid if unspectacular job in Eustace's establishment in Hong Kong. Eustace needed, said the letter, a man who was trustworthy and diligent and he was very keen that Edson join him.

'Trustworthy and diligent,' repeated Edson slowly. 'Almost a hundred years old, the most respected timber business in the region, even the country. And now Eustace wants me because I am 'trustworthy and diligent'! He hardly knows me! It's just pity. And the sad thing is that it makes sense for me to accept it.'

Tehmina squeezed Edson's arm. 'He remembers you. Or at least he remembers what you were. He remembers that you supported him when the rest of the family sniggered at his dreams. Life is full of little pay-offs for our forgotten goodnesses. It is gratitude, not pity. It makes sense for us to go. I am not sure I will like it much, but I will be there.' She sighed and cast her arm around, 'All this is... so important to me. But if leaving will take away the sadness that I see in you every day then we should at least try.'

'Yes,' said Edson reflectively. 'I think it is the most sensible thing to do. At least we can try it out for a few months. We will have a word with Phil about it.'

'I don't see any problem there. She is obsessed with bouncing from one thing to another. She will jump at it.'

'What about that boy of hers? These things usually matter.'

142

'To normal people, yes. To Phil, I don't know. Anyway, things seem to have gone off the boil lately,' said Tehmina, a hint of satisfaction in her voice. 'Lancelot seems to like his job in London, so it is unlikely that he will come back at all. Steady boy!' said Tehmina gratefully.

The next morning Edson and Tehmina were continuing the discussion over breakfast when Philomena sauntered in.

'What's all the talk about, then?' asked Philomena casually.

Edson told her about the offer from his cousin.

'Wonderful,' said Philomena dryly, 'and what will you be? Assistant manager? Chief manager? And you can always go to the Indian gymkhana and chat with the grocers. Wonderful! At least it will be a change.'

Encouraged by this last comment, Tehmina said: 'Exactly! Nothing is happening in the business here, anyway.'

Edson nodded in agreement. 'It's a new order,' he said, 'run by people I cannot understand. At least Hong Kong is still...' He stopped himself too late.

'Ah!' said Philomena, grinning broadly. *That's* the attraction. Lots of lovely English accents to listen to and talk with! And *The Times* will only be a week old instead of the month-old copies you read here.' Still smiling, she shook her head slowly. 'Do you know what you are? You're a dinosaur, a colonial junkie!' She shrugged her shoulders. 'Well, good luck to you.'

'We were wondering what you would do there,' said Tehmina.

'Oh, don't worry about me – I am leaving too.'

Her parents leaned forward expectantly. Philomena smiled at them with the air of a magician about to unveil the *pièce de résistance*. 'I am going to Africa.'

Normally, announcements like that are met with amused tolerance by parents. But Tehmina and Edson knew their daughter too well to not be alarmed.

'Certainly not!' said Tehmina when she had finished spluttering. 'How? With whom? That Nestor fellow? Out of the question! We are not going to pay for this foolishness!'

'You don't have to,' said Philomena evenly. 'Nestor has got me some sort of job on a ship that leaves in two weeks.'

'Two weeks!? And how do propose to support yourself when you get there?' screeched Tehmina.

'We are going to his village. It is quite remote. I don't know… There is a UN mission in the village. Maybe they will give me some work, we'll see.'

Edson started hesitantly: 'Surely Hong Kong…'

'Hong Kong,' interjected Philomena, 'is not in my plans. I wish you well. Though I may think you a fool to live your life chasing the *Raj*, it is your life and I will respect your choices as you must respect mine.' She pushed the chair back firmly and strode to the door.

'Come back here!' Tehmina screamed after her. 'I absolutely forbid it!'

Philomena stopped at the door and turned around. 'You know, I really think you would have been happier if I had stayed blind. You would have been able to mould me into whatever made *you* happy. Perfectly happy.' She swept out of the room.

Tehmina quivered with rage. She turned on Edson. 'There are limits. You must stop this!'

Edson shook his head slowly. 'I cannot understand where all this rebellion came from. I am not like that, nor you.'

Tehmina bit her lip. The fight seemed to suddenly go out of her. 'You must stop her,' she repeated dully, the vehemence gone.

Those were tense days. Philomena instructed Nestor to stay away from the house. She made her arrangements quietly, doing her best to be unobtrusive. Her mother finally realised that Edson would not stop her, and that no amount of ranting would move him to impose himself. She shrieked at the servants, at Philomena, at Zarthushtra himself at the fire temple. She tried to reason with Philomena, then entice her to go with them to Hong Kong, and finally, despairingly, to emotionally blackmail her. When she burst into tears as Philomena walked into the house laden with things to take with her Philomena did feel a pang of sorrow. She continued to her room without a word.

Edson and Tehmina were also due to leave, and Tehmina threw herself into the organisation of their departure and the care of the house during their absence with hysterical determination, desperate to erase the pain of her failure to reverse Philomena's decision. Sawant, who had been appointed caretaker, was bombarded with instruction after instruction. Alamai was to be in overall charge and Sawant was to report to her periodically. Edson made the illegal arrangements for the transfer of his dwindling resources to Hong Kong, a process that served to fortify his decision to leave. He put in place the legal formalities for the disposal of his estate in the event of his not returning.

The day before Philomena was to leave, Tehmina entered her room. Seeing Philomena's things strewn all over the room, she burst into tears again.

'For God's sake!' said Philomena, exasperated. 'I am only going for a while! Maybe I will join you in Hong Kong later, maybe you will be back here, who knows?'

Tehmina wiped her eyes with the back of her hand. She held out a small box to Philomena. 'It is for you. To keep your things in.'

Philomena looked at the silver filigree box. It had a small photo-frame set into the front with a photograph of the Queen in it. Philomena smiled to herself and opened the box. Inside it was a rough metal chain, hanging from which was a tarnished silver pendant in the shape of a fishing *dhow*. It looked old and neglected, but Philomena sensed that the dull green crust covered secrets, hid a history.

When Tehmina spoke again there was a gravity in her voice which hinted at her words having deeper meanings she could not dare to voice. 'Your father gave it to me long ago. I want you to have it. Do not tell Edson I gave it to you – it would only upset him. Wherever you go, look at it and you will know where you came from, where you belong.'

Tehmina took a half-step forward and made as if to touch her daughter. 'Be careful. Write to Alamai – we will exchange addresses through her.'

Philomena turned away. Putting on the necklace, she looked at herself in the mirror.

'It is very pretty,' she said.

Her tone did not betray that she was moved. She tossed the box onto a pile of things ready for packing. 'Thanks,' she said, heaving a trunk onto the bed.

Her mother hesitated a moment. Then she mumbled something about seeing to the clothes for the *dhobi* and left, streaming tears that Philomena did not want to turn and see.

At dinner that night there was the same sense of loss and fragmentation as when Lancelot had left India for Britain and when Britain had left India for Britain, only this time it was accentuated by the completeness of the coming disintegration. They talked about practical things: how long Philomena's voyage would take, where exactly Nestor's village was, how long it would take to get to the docks, the arrangements for Edson and Tehmina in Hong Kong, how Philomena should steer clear of the political shambles in Nestor's country. Now that the moment was upon them, practicality kicked in and a precarious rational equilibrium prevailed. The final unravelling of the DaCruz family washed about the room, painstakingly ignored by its creators.

# Twenty

Philomena stepped off the steamer onto the dusty quay. There was a new definition to her body: the sinews were taut, her belly hard and flat from long steamy days hauling clothes in the laundry room, cleaning, washing, putting her body to work. Her skin gleamed, gold-plated, and her step was strong and lithe.

The journey had been a blur. They had both been made to work hard and long. Nestor taught Philomena the basics of his language, and she quickly achieved a fair level of proficiency. The crew had been entranced by Philomena, but it was the captain himself, a wart-marked old rogue from Alexandria, who had attracted Philomena. They spent long, intoxicated hours talking, the captain recounting his improbable experiences and outrageous conquests. Their meetings became the topic of jocular conversations amongst the crew and Nestor joined in happily.

The first night she slept with the captain, Philomena returned to her bunk in the early hours. As she quietly let herself down onto the bed in the dark, Nestor asked what time she had been mustered for the next day and whether she wanted him to wake her. Philomena was surprised that Nestor was awake, and a little pleased. But as she answered him she found herself irritated by the bland indifference she had noticed in his tone and resolved to not let it bother her in future. It was much, much later that Nestor stopped staring into the darkness and slept.

But in general, relations between them on the voyage had been amicable. Philomena thought she had stopped expecting Nestor to react to her actions and Nestor thought he had stopped expecting anything at all from her.

*

The afternoon of their arrival, Philomena and Nestor strolled through the streets and markets of the city. Piles of okra, small baskets of aubergines, great big heaps of mangoes and plantains and pepper and pineapples flashed into and out of Philomena's sight between the riotous colours of the local's batik clothing. She drank copious cups of whatever was on offer – the fiery ginger drink that every second person seemed to be peddling. flowery *bissap,* and tea of all temperatures and hues.

Slowly, Philomena's attention was drawn to the one thing other than the piles of onions that were steadfastly brown among all this colour. The onions she knew, but the long brown tubes stacked high at every stall were a mystery. She veered off and pushed through the crowd to one of the stalls. The lady behind the stall glanced away from the customer she was serving momentarily, then started back and grinned at Philomena.

'What is that?' asked Philomena.

'Cassava! That is cassava!' the lady beamed.

Cassava! Images of her geography textbook in school jumped to mind. The staple of half the world! And still unknown in India. She picked up one of the brown tubes.

'How much?' she asked.

'One?' the woman said, holding up one finger and grinning.

Philomena nodded. The woman burst into laughter, then waved her away.

Philomena smiled and thanked her. She examined the cassava, and turning away, made to bite into it. She heard the howl from behind her a split second before she found herself being upended and landing heavily in the dust with the vegetable seller beside her. The woman was shouting at her in a language she did not understand.

Drawn by the commotion, Nestor had pushed his way through the crowd.

'Should have known...' he said, smiling.

Helping Philomena up, he spoke quietly to the woman who answered in a trembling voice, clearly still agitated. Nestor started laughing softly. The woman stopped and stared at him, then slowly started chuckling herself.

'You'd better thank her,' said Nestor.

'What for?'

Nestor picked up the cassava and held it up.

'I've already thanked her for that! But if she...'

Nestor turned to the woman and spoke to her briefly. He took Philomena by the arm. She smiled uncertainly at the woman as they left.

'What?' asked Philomena

'That bite you were about to take? It could have killed you. Cassava is poisonous. Full of cyanide. Has to be drained and carefully prepared to be safe to eat.'

'Ah,' said Philomena softly as she glanced fearfully at another pile of strange-looking things at a stall they were passing.

Nestor followed her gaze and chuckled softly. 'Mangosteen,' he said. 'Quite nice. Want to try?'

'It's okay, I'm fine,' muttered Philomena uncertainly.

*

That night, Nestor took Philomena through the deserted streets of the capital. They walked a long time, coming across few people. Stray dogs barked and howled, somehow always in the distance. At every street corner they came across the shadowy figures of soldiers and policemen leaning on walls or traffic signals that guided no traffic. Finally they turned into a dark alley, halfway down which Nestor stepped into an entrance lit by a single, dim light bulb.

They entered a huge room, the darkness of which could not be dispelled by the hundreds of candles that flickered on the walls and on the rough wooden tables around which people sat drinking. It could have been enchanting, this golden bar. But bars have happy, rowdy people in them; laughing, shouting, singing. Here, they sat in the flickering light talking in whispers, as if aware that they were losing the battle against becoming a part of the forces of the night.

Nestor glanced around the tavern. He looked tense, alert. Philomena followed him to a small table by a rough stone wall covered with wax drippings from the candles stuck on it.

'What's the matter?' she asked.

'Nothing,' said Nestor, his eyes continuing to flick around the room as he spoke.

Philomena persisted. 'Is there something about this place I should know?'

Nestor leaned forward, his voice low and urgent. 'There is something about *every* place here you should know about – nobody knows who the next person may turn out to be. Talk very little, drink a lot, and *never* stare at anyone.'

'Sounds pretty morbid. Why are we here at all? Isn't there...' Philomena voice trailed off. From a table in the corner across the room, a man with half a face was staring intently at them. Looking closer, she could see that the missing half of his face seemed to consist of craters, like a moonscape with an eye stuck in it. She told Nestor and saw him stiffen.

'Is he alone?'

'There's someone else with him wearing a hat, but he has his back to us.'

Nestor rose abruptly from his chair. 'I'll get something to drink,' he said.

As he walked to the counter at the far end of the room, the man in the hat seemed to turn his head a fraction in Nestor's direction. The crater-faced man rose and followed Nestor to the counter. Standing beside Nestor he seemed to say something. Nestor did not appear to notice. He returned with the glasses of beer, looking preoccupied.

'I think it is better if we drink up and leave,' he said.

Philomena nodded weakly, and Nestor was momentarily amused by the worry on her face. They talked no further, Philomena concentrating on draining her drink, while Nestor's attention seemed to wander off again. As they rose to leave Philomena glanced over at the table in the far corner. It was empty.

Out on the dark streets, Philomena asked 'So who were they?'

'Who was who?' asked Nestor. He seemed far away.

'The men. In the bar.'

'Ah. I'm not sure, really. Maybe... Then again, maybe they are... I'll... I don't know. Let's see.'

Turning the corner, they froze. Silhouetted by a dreary street lamp was the profile of a policeman, pistol cocked and pointing steadily at a dark bundle up against the wall of a building. A shot rang out and a screaming rat detached itself from the bundle and dragged itself past where they stood, trailing its gut behind it.

Chuckling to himself, the policeman turned and strolled away across the street. Philomena lit a cigarette and noticed her hands were trembling. No lights went on, nobody stirred in the darkened windows of the houses along the street.

As they slipped into their room Nestor said that he had to go out again.

No, please, just stay with me, thought Philomena. 'Okay,' she said, shrugging her shoulders.

She went over to the window and watched Nestor walk away down the dim street into the shadows. If anything happened to him she would be alone here, utterly alone. It was a new feeling and it ruthlessly stripped her bravado bare. There were no comforting support systems that could be taken for granted here, no implicit understanding of the nuances of the environs.

She curled up in her bed and turned out the light. Somehow the darkness made her feel more secure, a little more not there. When Nestor returned she pretended to be asleep.

*

Nestor walked quickly through the empty streets, treading as lightly as he could, trying to be unobtrusive amongst the empty pavements and dreary street lights. He passed the dead rodent the policeman had shot, then turned into a dark, narrow lane and then another.

He stopped outside the address the man at the bar had given him. The night was cool, but Nestor found himself wiping his brow. If the men at the bar were the opposition and resistance, he wanted to know more. If they were secret police, he had no option but to follow their instructions anyway. He knocked on the dirty door the way he had been instructed.

The door opened a crack. A hand reached out, grabbed his collar and yanked him in. The door close softly as he was pushed against a wall. A torch shone in his face as he was frisked.

'It's alright,' said a voice.

Dim lights came on, and he saw a crumbling room with a table in the centre.

'Sit,' said the man in the hat, who was already seated at the table.

As Nestor moved to the table, he saw that it had been the man with the mooncrater face who had frisked him.

The man in the hat stared at Nestor, saying nothing.

'Sir, who are you, sir? Why do you want to see me?' asked Nestor.

More silence. Then, 'You can call me Leon,' said the man in the hat. 'Central Security Guard'. He slid an ID card across the table.

Nestor merely glanced at it. To pick it up would be seen as a challenge to their word.

He felt a chill rise in his body. The CSG. But why here? Why this strange dingy room? Why has he just not been called to the Jackfruit Factory?

'Because if we had taken you to headquarters we would have needed to leave a record of this... encounter,' said Leon.

He's lying, thought Nestor. Most of the people taken to those headquarters disappeared. No question of records. The rumour was that the streets at the back of the building stank like jackfruit from the corpses that were constantly being loaded into lorries through the rear gates.

'Oh yes, there are,' said Leon, reading Nestor's thoughts again. 'There are files for everyone there. We thought it best in your case that there should be nothing at all.'

Nestor rubbed his chin to prevent a hanging bead of sweat from falling.

'Now. You will tell us how you paid for your time in India.'

'The fees aren't much,' said Nestor. 'That's why there are a lot of students from poor countries there. And I used to do odd jobs, reading to the handicapped, selling toys...'

'No!' shouted Leon. He leaned forward and snarled 'You will tell us what we don't know, not what we already do! Do you understand?'

'Sir, there is nothing to tell. Really. Nothing at all, sir,'

'You received money. From whom?'

'From home, sir.'

'We know what you received from home! You couldn't feed a dog on that!'

'Nothing else, sir. Really, sir.'

Leon pushed a piece of paper towards Nestor. He took a pen out of his pocket and flung it down.

'Write! Names, dates, amounts if you can remember. But most important, from where. I will give you three minutes to remember. And to write.'

'But sir, you know everything, every movement of mine!'

Moonface burst out, 'You think it's that easy! Everyone doesn't help us. The bastards don't let us work –'

Leon turned sharply and glared and Moonface fell silent.

So they really didn't know anything, really weren't sure! It wasn't just a grotesque game to test him.

Leon turned back and ceremonially placed his watch on the table, never once looking away from Nestor's face.

Nestor stared back. His eyes flicked down to the watch. It was digital, but somehow he could hear the ticking of time. He shook his head and looked up.

Leon leaned over to Moonface and whispered in his ear. Moonface went to a dusty telephone in a corner of the room behind the table and made a phone call.

'Please sir…'

'Not much time left,' said Leon.

'I have nothing more to give you. Really, Sir!'

Leon sighed. Reaching into his jacket, he pulled out a gun and carefully placed it on the table in front of him.

'You have your father's stubbornness in you.' He smiled. 'Look where that got him. Think carefully. A nation's peace and prosperity flows out of the barrel of a gun. Revolt is a crime. Be good. Tell me.'

Nestor remained silent.

'My friend has just confirmed with our associates. The lady you arrived with? We have her. And with one more call we can make her disappear.' He snapped his fingers. 'Just like that.'

Nestor thought furiously, but he knew somewhere inside him what the answer was always going to be. After a long while, he said, 'So be it.'

Leon looked over at Moonface, who moved over to Nestor, grabbed his right arm and slammed it down on the table in front of him. He spread the hand palm down on the table. From his pocket he took a large wicked-looking nail and a hammer.

Good, thought Nestor to himself. The gambit about Phil was a fake, just a test.

'Do you know what killed Jesus, Musambe?' asked Leon.

Nestor was silent, his mind and body working in preparation for what was to come.

Moonface carefully placed the point of the nail in the middle of Nestor's hand.

'Loss of blood? Heatstroke? Plain and simple pain from being nailed to the cross?' continued Leon. 'Yes, a nail through the hand will pain, but not enough to break a stubborn mule like Jesus. Or you. There's not enough in that part of the body to kill you. Not even to cause enough pain.'

He nodded to Moonface, who now moved the nail up Nestor's hand to rest in the middle of the base of his middle finger.

'Now the fingers... Nails driven through the bone at the right place... Hurts just as much, but the hand also becomes useless – after we've done all five, that is.'

Leon leaned forward, his eyes boring into Nestor. 'Suffocation. Jesus died of suffocation. In that position you can't breathe.'

'And,' said Nestor slowly, 'his executioners were animals. Like all of you.'

'We only do our job. Protecting the people.' Leon nodded to Moonface, who raised the hammer.

Nestor stared straight into Leon's eyes. 'And who will protect you when the time comes?'

Leon stared back at him a moment, then his face

crinkled into a smile. He began to laugh, and Nestor heard Moonface join in. Moonface slipped his implements back into his pocket and slapped Nestor on the back.

Leon got up and came round to Nestor, arms open. Nestor got shakily to his feet.

'Welcome home,' said Leon. 'Come, sit. There is much to be done.'

They sat down at the table, and the other two gave Nestor a rundown on the government: its structure, its procedures, its record, its repression, its excesses. Nestor already knew a fair amount about the government but there were details and incidents they told him of which made his blood run cold.

'Why me?' he asked.

Leon smiled. 'Because we will need stubborn mules when the time comes.'

'Now, about this girl, we have considered the options and decided that she must go with you. In some ways it would have been neater to have arranged for an accident to have befallen her, but she may well provide some useful diversionary cover. Take her with you. There is a UN outpost in the village run by a woman called Carla. Convince her to apply to her bosses that the girl be taken on to assist her. We will do the rest.'

'Can I think about it?' said Nestor.

Leon smiled again. 'You already have for many months now, haven't you? You are too intelligent to not have analysed the situation here, so once the decision to return had been taken there was never any other choice, was there?'

'Sorry about the little drama. We just needed to make sure you were ready,' said Moonface. 'Here, you can join the oppressors, which you don't have in you, or you can become the oppressed, which is not in your blood.' He drew the rusty nail from his pocket. 'You have already chosen to fight, Nestor.'

Without waiting for Nestor to respond Leon proceeded to give him names of contacts and brief him on the procedure he should follow. When he had finished he held out his hand to Nestor.

As they shook hands a smile played on Leon's lips. 'Much great poetry has come out of bloodshed. Do not desert your first love.'

# Twenty-one

A regular mobile buffet, this bus, thought Philomena. She could not remember ever having eaten so much fruit, or seen so many sticky, smiley faces. And then there were the hawkers at the window at every stop – eggs, *kose*, bread, *wageshi* cheese...

A man carrying an evil-looking machete beamed at her and offered her a chunk of pineapple, and she wistfully wondered why nature had bestowed upon her a yellowing, western set of teeth.

By eleven in the morning they had been rattling along for four hours with, according to Nestor, another four to go. The feasting had started soon after they had set off, and the flow of food and the merriment of the travellers conspired to make Philomena almost forget what Nestor had told her about his meeting with the men the night before.

The bus stopped from time to time as people clambered on and off. The dense coastal forests gradually

161

succumbed to woodlands, and the woodlands to grass and scrub. Twice they were halted by soldiers who rummaged roughly through the luggage, pocketing things that caught their fancy. An elderly lady in the seat in front of Nestor sat motionless as a soldier casually snatched away the chicken she had cradled in her lap all journey. Then he turned and stared hard at Philomena, and she felt her lip begin to twitch. She drew it back over her lip. Something told her to look down. It worked. The soldier seemed to lose interest.

As the bus moved off Nestor leaned over and spoke quietly with the lady.

'What?' asked Philomena.

'Nothing. Well… nothing unusual, anyway. She sold a bit of land, and went to the city and bought some things, including that chicken for her grandson's birthday. He hasn't tasted it before and he is not going to now either. Cigarette?'

Nestor offered a cigarette to the lady. She took one. Then she hesitated and took another, grinning broadly and vigorously nodding her head in thanks. She tucked away one of the cigarettes deep in the recesses of her damp blouse, lit the other, and commenced a detailed inquiry into the prospects of her working in India, guffawing jovially at the thought during gaps in the conversation.

Philomena gradually dropped out of the conversation, her belly full. She gazed out of the window of the bus. The landscape had changed. It looked grimmer, the soft edges left behind somewhere. The hard sun singed vast, gutted spaces where fields and people and life should have been. Occasionally they passed convoys of soldiers and armoured cars. The people on the bus did not seem to notice.

Philomena was just dropping off to sleep when a series of explosions went off in the distance. The lady, who was still talking to Nestor, allowed her eyes to flicker away out of the window for a second before resuming her conversation. None of the others seemed to take any notice. Philomena looked across to Nestor anxiously. He caught her eye, smiled comfortingly and continued to talk to the lady. Moments later, Philomena dozed off in the heavy afternoon heat.

It was a travel sleep, full of strange dreams and dozy awakenings. Once, between naps, she had opened her eyes and seen the tangled wreck of a tank. As the bus moved past it, the gun turret came into view. Hanging neatly along it were bright gold and blue and red batik garments drying in the sun. The explosions still rumbled in the distance. She drifted off to sleep again, smiling to herself.

The journey went on. The chicken lady, lost in conversation with Nestor, missed her stop and suddenly screeched to the driver to stop. She shouted her goodbyes to the bus and tumbled out, cheerily cuffing the conductor on his back on the way. The balance of movement shifted in favour of getting off, till Nestor and Philomena were the only ones left on the bus.

The bus stopped again. Philomena peered through the swirling dust at a couple of ramshackle abandoned structures by the road. No hawkers, no bus stop. There did not seem to be anyone around. She turned to Nestor questioningly.

'End of the road. We get off here. Beyond this is rebel territory.' Philomena noted a hint of satisfaction in Nestor's voice. 'And the punishment for being rebel territory is no buses, no roads, no electricity.' Nestor rose from his seat. 'Well,' he said softly. 'We shall see.'

As they alighted, the conductor unloaded several large jerrycans of fuel from the bus. Then he hopped onto the footboard of the bus and flung a bundle of mail into the dust by the cans. Leaving Philomena, Nestor and jerrycans standing there, the bus turned around and disappeared back down the road they had just travelled.

They stood and listened to the sound of the engine being slowly drowned out by the silence, and Philomena discovered for the first time what complete and absolute silence sounded like. No wind to rustle the absent leaves. Not even the flap of a wing or the cry of an insect. Nothing moved. Nestor turned to look around and the scrunch of his pivoting shoe intruded upon the moment.

Parked by the side of one of the structures was a battered Land Rover with its bonnet open, a pair of jeans bent over it. A tool clinked under the bonnet. Philomena found the sound strangely reassuring. They walked towards the jeans, the scrunch of their footsteps continuing to defile the air.

As they near the car, a voice from inside the bonnet said: 'Nestor, is it?'

'Yes, sir,' said Nestor hesitantly.

'You see those cans that came with you? Bring them here.' The voice was gruff, but distinctly female.

'Yes ma'am,' said Nestor, correcting himself.

As he finished ferrying the fuel across, the woman

164

pulled herself out from under the bonnet, and turned and gazed upon Nestor and Philomena. She stuck out a grease-laden hand. 'Carla Kokushka,' she said curtly, but the wrinkles around her eyes were honest and warm.

'Right. Empty one of those into the tank and load the others in the back,' she directed, addressing neither of them in particular. Wiping her hands on her jeans, she watched Nestor fill the diesel into the car. As she turned away to shut the bonnet she said: 'There is no way I can make that fat bastard pay for the diesel, or I would – he has made me come here three days in a row to meet you and take you back to the village. So I suppose the UN will just have to pay.'

She slammed the bonnet shut much harder than necessary and a man who had been sleeping in the back seat of the car jumped suddenly into view. He looked around sleepily till his gaze fell upon Nestor. The man flung the door open and charged towards Nestor, who was already charging forward himself. They collided violently, hugging each other and yowling, till Nestor stumbled on a rock and fell to the ground, taking Milton with him. They got slowly to their feet, laughing and dusting themselves off.

Carla watched the performance, hands on hips. 'Come on, beautiful,' she said, sweeping up a jerrycan in each hand with surprising ease. As she swung them into the back of the vehicle she said: 'Remember to never rely upon a man. Thoroughly useless, the lot of them.'

She turned to Philomena, 'You are in front with me,' she directed crisply. 'You two, you are in the back with the diesel – I know it's not the cleanest car in the world,

165

but if you're going to carry half the dust in Africa on your clothes you can sit in the back with the other rubbish.'

They drove on dirt tracks and over open land. Carla explained to Philomena that there were four other UN representatives spread over the rebel-held region fighting a losing battle to ensure that the government did not succeed in completely destroying the people there. She told her that Nestor's village had been relatively untouched and prosperous, and nobody quite understood why this was so. She told Philomena of how Milton had worked himself up into a frenzy over Nestor's return, and how he was terrified that Nestor would join the ranks of the rebels and be lost to him again. They talked about how the military made periodic pushes into the region, how they launched random and brutal attacks on villages. The rebels were well organised too, and had repeatedly succeeded in destroying bridges and communications, and even the occasional army post. Some time back the government had launched a major operation in the area only to find the resistance embarrassingly strong. They had hastily reconsidered their strategy and decided to contain the insurgency within a defined region. Carla herself had been harassed and impeded in her work at every stage. The authorities reasoned that if she worked in the area, she had to know more about the rebels than she had been willing to tell them. In their eyes, that made her a collaborator with some vague sort of diplomatic immunity.

Philomena asked if Carla could find her some work, and Carla smiled grimly and said 'plenty'. Philomena could start with helping her out, and she would see what she could do about getting her an UN identity card. It was a priceless document: though both sides hated the UN 'meddlers', they reluctantly left them alone.

As the sun began to set Carla pointed to a knob of huts on a rise in the distance. Abutting it to the right was a hill capped by an almost perfect globe. Carla confirmed that it was indeed the fabled Akimbo's Head. As she spoke the constant stream of banter and giggling that had accompanied them from the rear of the car seem to fade. Philomena looked around. Nestor's eyes were transfixed upon the distant rise. He had fallen silent, and all the expression had shifted into his eyes.

When they reached the rise and started their bumpy ascent to the village a gaggle of children whooped towards the car. Carla brought the vehicle to a halt for a few seconds and the children piled on. Philomena noticed that each one had his or her own appointed bit of footboard or bonnet or window to hang onto. It was obviously a well-established routine.

Carla drove on at a crawl. 'They love it, and it's harmless,' said Carla, making a face at a boy perched on the bonnet. 'Though Millie who lives over there,' she said, nodding towards a thatched hut they were passing, 'says that to sit in this thing is to sell your spirit to the unnatural forces of motors and machines.'

There was no particular pattern to Carla's progress through the village: there was no main road, no rows of houses, no marketplace to define her path. She weaved around mud houses and the attached little vegetable gardens that each one seemed to have, over bumpy open spaces, finally coming to a halt outside a semi-permanent structure made of modern materials, a little bigger and much uglier than the others. She caught Philomena's look of disapproval and explained apologetically that she needed to protect the stores and the medicine from the rain and the heat.

Carla pointed past where they had stopped. 'You see the last hut there high up at the top of the rise, a little apart from the others? That's Nestor's.'

Nestor and Milton sprang out of the car and disappeared between some huts, hooting like liberated schoolchildren. The joyriders also jumped off their perches – the vehicle was of no interest to them when stationary.

Watching them disappear, Carla said dryly: 'No one seems to be in any hurry to get home, it appears. Come on in and have some wine.'

They sat amongst stores with improbable names like 'Denmark' and 'USA' stamped on their packaging, talking and drinking an ancient and ferocious palm wine made from baobab pods. As daylight drifted further and further away into the distant sky, Philomena could feel that Carla wanted to say something. Twice she seemed to start, only to shy away at the last moment. They sat in the shadows, not speaking, till finally Carla leaned forward and banged down her cup, peering hard at Philomena.

'There is an old saying here: "Fear is no obstacle to death".' She looked away. 'Revolt can be a drug. Nestor will take to it. I know, I can feel it,' she said. Philomena smiled and considered telling Carla about the men in the bar. 'You can either take to it too, or fight it and count your losses in bitterness. Either way, you will lose.'

Philomena smiled. 'Revolt is not exactly alien to me.'

Carla sighed and looked away out of the window. When she spoke again, she sounded as if she was far away. 'You know nothing of it.'

Philomena stood up. 'I should go,' she said.

As she walked away towards Nestor's house, the lantern Carla had given her in one hand and a bag in the other, Carla called out after her. 'Preserve yourself! This is no place to nurture private loves.'

Philomena climbed the path that led up to the clearing and Nestor's solitary hut, her head full of palm wine and gun-turret clothes lines and predictions of loss. Setting down the lantern, she walked around the hut in the weak moonlight. Someone had recently tended to the little vegetable patch at the back of the hut, and neat rows of tiny sprigs sprouted from the ground. She peered in through a rough opening that served as a window and was surprised to find the inside spotless and tidy. She discovered later that Milton and his son had spent days doing up the hut for Nestor's return.

She went back to the clearing in front. Lighting the lantern, she lay down on the ground wondering at the stars above and around her, almost beside her. She could see them in the gap between her feet, perching on her shoulders, resting on her reclining breasts. A cool wind began to blow. Her world of buildings and cars and streets had hidden away the world's true size, protected its inhabitants from seeing how little they really were. She shuddered and looked towards the path for Nestor,

169

but there was no comforting bob of light. She got up and walked quickly towards the hut, away from the vastness. One day she would come to love it, but at this moment she needed the hut; its shape, its connections to man and his work.

The wind changed direction, and as she leaned against the reassuring roughness of the wall she could hear Nestor and Milton's voices drifting across to her from Akimbo's Head. Little flickering lights from the village pushed their way through the darkness. Reassured by the sounds of the men, Philomena sat and listened to the contented chorus of the night insects. Tired and drowsy, she should have fallen asleep, but sleep would not come.

Eventually she heard them approach. They carried no light: they did not seem to need one. They had retrieved the luggage from Carla, and Philomena took her things and went into the hut.

She lay down on the floor listening to the two men outside recovering missing bits from each other's lives. Sleep remained elusive. Her mind was restless, and she tossed about uneasily, like a guest in an unfamiliar bed with unknown pillows and alien sheets.

Why had Carla said they could not love here? It was true that as she had watched Nestor walk towards the hut, she had noticed a new strength in Nestor's walk, a new purpose of movement, a new power in his body. There were inflections in his speech she had never heard before. Even before she could actually see the change, she had been able to close her eyes and sense his being changing, the air around him tightening into steely, resolute cords, squeezing out lingering pockets of vagrant air. This was a man she did not know and had never possessed. A formidable, attractive man. And it was here, in the midst of the crusade that she knew he would dedicate himself to, in this land that Carla had warned her had no time for tenderness, that Philomena realised that she was a little in love again. Or had she merely been aroused again by this new man who had nothing to do with her Nestor? And if she offered him her hunger again why should he accept this tainted offering? He had watched it fade so easily before. No, she would have to make him love her not with the casual carnality of the past but in some new, more substantial way. The awareness deep down in her that she had no idea at all about how to do this frightened and unsettled her.

# Twenty-two

Some months later, Nestor left for a brief while, saying he needed to meet some people who were doing, in his words, 'important work'. As time passed, the trips became more frequent, and his absences longer.

One day, Milton and his son Titi walked over to the clearing outside the hut, where Philomena was attempting to put together a table from some pieces of wood.

'When will he be back?' he asked.

'Soon, I should think. He said this was going to be a short one,' she replied. 'Beer?'

Milton's chest heaved as he nodded and sank heavily onto a chair that Nestor and Philomena had built together. Despite working his little field every day and trying hard to be both father and lost mother to his son, Milton was not a fit man. Clearly overweight, he rarely walked great distances like the others all seemed to, except on his weekly visits to his wife's grave a few miles away, and his midriff prominently preceded him on the journey.

'Do *you* approve of what he is doing?' asked Milton as Philomena returned with the drink.

Philomena shrugged. 'He thinks it's right. That's good enough for me.'

'Right? It's only right if you actually get somewhere with it! Why should we believe that things will be any better if the rebels succeed? The only reason why the tribes are not tearing each other to pieces within the movement is because they have a common foe for the moment.' Milton fell silent. 'Try and convince him. It will not be difficult to get some land for him to work. You can build something together.'

Philomena sighed quietly. 'I can only influence his choices if I can make him care about me, and I am afraid I have never given him much reason to.'

Milton seemed irritated. 'You are as enthusiastic about this as he is, aren't you? I don't know you well, but I see the hold his obsession has upon you. You think it is glamorous, don't you? You are both fools – he chases the dream, you chase the glamour! All this rebellion, it only ever brings pain in the end. Sooner or later, there is death. Nothing changes. Dream over. And all that's left for you to put your arms around is the glamour. Why not just try and live a life? God knows that's difficult enough! Build something *positive*, only for yourselves.'

Milton noticed a hint of distress in Philomena's eye.

'I'm sorry,' he continued, 'but I've seen all this so often. He is still only going to meetings, being trained,

173

getting to know the organisation – that's what you do for the first year or two. But soon he will start out on operations. He will believe he's fighting for a cause and slowly forget that he is fighting for his life. The longer it goes on, the more difficult and uncertain it will be and then you will not be able to tell me when you expect him back.' Milton leaned forward and grabbed Philomena's hand urgently. 'Ask him to stop. Beg him! You *must*!'

Philomena sighed. 'You have come to the wrong person. My particular field of expertise has always been *not* listening to anyone.'

After a while Philomena asked hesitantly, 'When they go on a mission... how does one know if... how it has gone?'

Milton slumped back in the chair. 'When they come back, you know. And when they do not come back, then also you know, except that you never know when exactly to stop expecting them to come back.' Milton turned and noticed his son fiddling with Nestor's cartridge belt. 'Leave that alone!' he snapped.

Milton turned back to Philomena. 'When did all this happen? When did this rebel appear?' asked Milton, almost inaudibly, as if to himself.

Philomena felt sorry for Milton. He was obviously trying to make Nestor fit into some scheme he had drawn up for their lives, to will back a vanished balance. 'I think I knew on the boat that it was on his mind. Just the little things he said. It was as though he was steeling himself, rearranging his thinking.' She started to tell Milton of the meeting with the men in the bar in the city, but Nestor had already told him.

Milton spoke again, almost in a whisper. 'It happened to all of us when we were at university. I resisted, a lot of the others did not. It starts with an ideal. Then it spreads, flourishes, eats away at the normal things in life, like friendships and loves. It fills you with this sense of higher purpose, then it corrodes and finally snaps your ties with others. Then it breaks your compassion and in the end your conscience. Everything is right, justifiable. No matter how brutal, how violent. In the end there is always the same sad, wasted rubble. Do you know why? Because nothing beautiful was ever created out of hatred.'

Darkness gathered in. A lingering purple slash in the sky was all that was left of the day. Philomena lit a lantern and they sat in silence. Milton's brooding was beginning to seep into Philomena when they heard the scrunch of Nestor's footsteps on the path.

As he came into the lamplight, they saw that his face looked flushed and alive, content in its sense of purpose. He slapped Milton heartily on the back and sat down beside him. Milton greeted him dully. Nestor drained a half-finished cup of beer and wiped his mouth with the back of his hand. Looking around, his eyes settled on Milton. 'Someone died?' he asked, smiling.

Milton looked away without speaking.

'Oh no, not that again!' said Nestor.

Milton seemed to consider Nestor's reaction for a moment. Then he pulled himself up and started to walk away towards the darkness. He stopped and turned around. From the waist up, he was covered in darkness. He pointed at Nestor, his fingertip shining golden in the light. 'It is all right to do all this if the only one who gets hurt is yourself.'

Nestor grinned blandly.

'Then die if you want to!' said Milton's voice from the shadows.

They sat still and silent as they listened to Milton's footsteps fade away. The lamplight on his legs, the golden finger, the voice from the darkness; it had felt like a prophecy, the hammer blows of an oracle. Philomena felt it, and she saw that Nestor had felt it too. A quiet shiver ran down her spine.

That night as Philomena slept, Nestor sat at the lamp outside writing the poetry he would not allow anyone to read.

# Twenty-three

As Milton had predicted, Nestor's apprenticeship ended soon after. He began to go on simple missions: carrying food into areas blockaded by the government, or stealing livestock or provisions from government farms and dumps. Simple things that could be explained away as hunger or ignorance if they were caught, acts which would attract nothing worse than a rifle butt in the stomach and a good kicking. He attended units meetings at which he discovered that Leon had been arrested and had disappeared. Moonface had just disappeared, without any intermediate formalities. Nestor found it strange that the others at the meeting used the word 'disappeared' with a kind of terminal acceptance and wondered if he himself would do the same as the days and years went by.

The clinical and ruthless efficiency with which Nestor executed his tasks quickly silenced any critics, and his rise through the ranks of the rebels was rapid and consistent. At the end of a year he was leading units into assignments of some delicacy, and the steady loss of his superiors in action ensured that he rapidly rose to a position of importance and responsibility within the militia. In the years that passed he developed a canniness and cunning that protected him from anything more serious than an occasional gash or narrow escape, while those around him stepped on mines he had somehow sensed were there and walked on paths that had whispered 'ambush' to him.

His absences became longer, his movements more erratic than ever. Close to seven years on from her arrival in Africa, it was Milton who shared the intimacy of Philomena's birth-giving with her. Nestor only saw his son when he returned to the village three days later.

All too soon, even his peers had been left by the wayside, and one evening he found himself being led over hills and across vast desert lakes to face the regional revolutionary council and be told he was now a part of them.

The regional council consisted of only four members, Nestor now included. Runners delivered instructions from the central council and carried reports back to it from time to time. The other three members formally introduced themselves: the greying old Hook (so named because of the unusual shape of his nose), Nestor had worked with occasionally and admired; Solomon, a small, silky man with a soft, sibilant manner of speech that hid a precise and cold-blooded understanding of tactical nuance; and Bene, a huge mountain of a man who could be a ferocious ally and a pitiless foe. They greeted him warmly: all three knew Nestor and must have expressed their approval of him to the central council. As they parted, Solomon whispered the details of their next meeting to Nestor.

Philomena slowly resigned herself to Nestor's absences. In the beginning she had waited anxiously for his return, silently deprecating herself for being concerned. But as the months turned to years and Nestor always returned, she stopped worrying about the possibility that he might not, like an airman's wife does. She nurtured a vegetable patch in the clearing with the stumbling but enthusiastic assistance of Christopher, their son. She spent long hours sitting on her haunches, watching Milton and Titi work the field and talking to Milton about trivial things she did not want to trouble Nestor with, like emotions and insecurities and hopes.

It was the day before Christopher's eighth birthday that she sat by the field watching Milton and Titi finish their work for the day. When he was done, Milton came over and sat beside her.

'So, where is Nestor today?' he asked.

'Oh, he's here. Working on some plan, or something.'

Milton glanced over at Philomena as she gazed at Titi and Christopher tumbling about together, giggling.

'And?'

'... and... and he's drifting away again. When Chris was born it changed. Just a bit. For a tiny bit. He seemed so happy to be involved. I mean, you could see he was trying. He still went away, but he told them he wanted to keep it a bit shorter, and did. And when he was back he was there with us every moment.'

'That's nice,' said Milton.

'One day he came back from a trip. Chris was so eager. He ran and leaped into his arms. Nestor swung him around in the air. They went off together so Nestor could wash up. When he'd finished, he wrung his wet hands all over Chris, who squealed and ran away. Nestor chased him, roaring. When he caught him, he lifted him onto his stomach as he lay down. They played for a while chuckling away to each other. As Christopher wriggled around, he slid off Nestor's stomach and fell to the floor, hitting his head heavily. Nestor sprung from the cot with a speed I had never seen before. He swept up Christopher and buried his head in his chest. Gently, he soothed the boy. For almost half an hour I'd say, till he finally fell asleep. He covered him gently, then turned swiftly and walked out of the door.

'I was a bit surprised by this, I'll admit. I followed him out. He sat in the clearing head in hands, and I could see his shoulders heaving. I went over to him.

'"He's fine. It wasn't your fault," I said, squeezing his shoulder.

'He turned slowly and looked at me. His face was wet "I know," he said dully. " It's not that, Phil." Then again softly, almost to himself, "It's not that." I sat down next to him. I could see he was struggling to talk about whatever it was.

'When he finally spoke his voice shook.

'"His face when he fell," he said. "It was the look on his face. I saw it before. Yesterday. In a village the army had attacked. We were to ambush their soldiers, but they changed their plan. We were too late. We walked through the village and got to a hut which had been completely gutted. It belonged to a family who had had helped one of our men. The whole family was there too. Strewn all over the place. And amongst the carnage, the body of a little boy. About…" Nestor pointed towards the hut, "… his age. And the look frozen on his face… the fear, the anxiety, it was just like on Christopher's as he fell just now." He was silent. After a long while he turned to me, his eyes pleading. "How do I reconcile all this, Phil? What do I do? How do I live these different lives?"

'I put my arm around in and held him, desperately hoping it would give him the answer I wanted him to find. And then I made the same old mistake. 'That is for you to decide, Nestor. That's your choice.'

Milton was silent. Philomena sighed and stood up.

'Come on,' she called to Christopher, 'It's time we got back home.'

Philomena and Christopher wound their way back up the path to the hut as the sun dropped low in the sky. Just as they reached the hut, something whirred past Christopher's ear. He shouted out in surprise and clung on to his mother.

'Helli-copter! Helli-copter!! The power to fly in your hands, kind sir!' roared Nestor, as he waltzed past them and retrieved the yellow plastic helicopter that he had launched.

'You brought that back from Bombay?'

'But of course, madam! Saved it for a special day!'

'Give it to me!' said Christopher.

181

'And how much will you pay me, sir?' asked his father. 'It's very expensive, this!'

Christopher looked confused.

'Only birthday boys can get this for free. Is it your birthday today, sir?'

'Yes. Almost. Tomorrow. Give me!'

'Aha, an advance present is it? Well... maybe if you can launch it further than me...'

'Easy!' shouted Christopher.

'Three chances,' said Nestor.

'Ten, you robber!' said Philomena.

'Five,' replied Nestor.

'Okay, eight. Final! Give me!' said the boy.

Nestor stood in front of Christopher, hands on hips. 'You drive a hard bargain, sir!' He scratched his chin, then said, 'Okay. It's a deal!'

Philomena watched smiling as they played. She cheered Christopher on as Nestor first taught him how to launch the helicopter and then let him win the contest.

When they were done, they went indoors to wash up. 'Aargh!' howled Nestor, in mock distress. 'My beautiful helli-copter! Stolen by this thief!

'Okay, okay. I'll give you a chance to try and win it back tomorrow. After my special birthday *oto* breakfast, when you will be too fat and full to launch it properly.'

'Good idea!' said Philomena.

Nestor's demeanour changed abruptly. He turned serious and ever so slightly apologetic.

'I... have to leave later tonight.'

Philomena turned away.

182

'Why?' cried Christopher. 'It's my birthday tomorrow!'

Nestor went over to Christopher. He scooped the boy in his arms and sat down with him in his lap.

'Tell me, son,' he said. 'Do you think I would rather be away at work or be with you on your birthday?'

'I don't know. Be with me?' asked Christopher tentatively.

'Yes. More than anything, always, I would want to be with you.'

'Then why not?' asked the boy.

'Because the work I do... the work I do is for you and for all the little children. To build a happy world for all of you. It's a big job, but someone has to do it. So if I miss one birthday, it's not so bad now, is it?

'I suppose,' said Christopher doubtfully.

'Do you trust me to do what's best?' asked Nestor.

Christopher nodded his head vigorously.

'Thank you. Then trust me. Please. It's for the good of all of us. I will be back in a couple of days. And if you don't practise hard with the helicopter, I will win it back from you,' he snapped his fingers 'like that!'

'Okay. Bet!'

'Bet.'

He left Christopher trying to snap his fingers and went out to where Philomena sat. She turned to look at him.

'I see your choice has been made,' she said.

'What can I do, Phil? What? What option do I have, Phil? I can sit here and till a field or something, and know that I have done nothing to make my son's world any better, this place any better. I know one thing, and one thing alone. I will fight to my last breath so I don't

183

leave my son the life that I have had. My dark... vagrant life. Struggling to win what any simple man should always have. Spurning his chances to build and live quietly, peacefully with those that love him.'

'The choice you mentioned that day, the day when Christopher fell off the bed? The choice of which life to lead? I thought about it so much, and there just seemed no answer. The face of the boy we'd found murdered, or the face of the boy who sat on my stomach and played? And then one day I realised they were both the same. I hadn't seen the true choice before me at all. And it is so simple. My life today, or my son's tomorrow. The answer was so obvious. There was nothing left to think about.'

'Even if you have to push away those who may matter the most to you?'

'That is not a choice I made, not something I have done, or wanted. If it happens, it is only a consequence. Something that I will have to bear.'

They sat in silence.

'Accursed land,' whispered Philomena.

Nestor jumped up and grinned. 'Fear not. The curse-lifters are at work!'

He turned and strode away.

*

Philomena smiled as Kanu spoke. Kanu always made her smile. Kanu, the grand old man who had lived in the village longer than anyone. He told her stories. Stories about the others in the village, moving from house to house and family to family. About Bura, who made the

184

haunting music Philomena often heard floating across from the village to her house in the still of night. How he played a broken *tambin*, the fracture in the flute itself imparting a special beauty to the music. He told her about the girl no one ever saw who lived alone in a hut ever so slightly outside the village because she had chosen to love unacceptably and failed. Now, her existence itself was only evidenced by the fact that her mother took her food and pigment from time to time and brought back livid painted fabric on the sales of which the family lived. Philomena remembered seeing the cloth, the images and patterns sometimes imperious and mocking, sometimes overwhelmed, broken. Then there were the boys who pretended to till their sterile land but ended up playing *mankala* all day, posting unencashable gains or unserviceable debts. This Philomena already knew about. She had played with them on one occasion and lost. When she returned the next day to discharge her debt they had stared at her in horror and directed her to join in the game in progress. When she refused they had accepted the payment with the greatest suspicion. Kanu laughed when she told him this. Nobody paid anybody, he said, but occasionally there was a tense game and sometimes an outstanding one. On such occasions the winner would invite everybody to a night of revelry at a nearby still, where an irascible but generous old hag churned out liquor from diverse dubious sources. The gamblers would all drink mightily, collectively running up formidable debts which none of them could pay. When the old shrew finally refused to serve them any more they would all

185

make furious calculations to work out who had lost the most. The loser would then have to persuade her that he possessed this or that valuable that he could sell in the city or convince her of his skill as a thief. Their patron treated both proposals even-handedly, clearly unconcerned by the exact legal status of the collateral offered. Kanu told Philomena about Jessica, who had for many years told everyone that she was only staying alive to see the day that her daughter found a job in Europe and left the village. If her wish were granted she would happily offer herself up to the Lord. In the most convoluted and illegal way, her daughter ultimately became a highly successful prostitute in Marseilles. As Jessica contentedly lay down to die she was disturbed by an irate and aggressive scorpion. Incensed by the insensitive intrusion upon this sublime moment, she battered the scorpion to death with gusto. Unfortunately, try as she might thereafter, she had never been able to recapture the moment again and had resigned herself to the prospect of remaining alive.

Carla had managed to wangle a small stipend for Philomena from the UN with little trouble, and Philomena flung herself into her work, leaving Christopher behind with Milton and Titi.

Every morning they would review things and exchange notes about the previous day – places most likely to fall victim to epidemics, areas the crops had failed in, villages that could be helped, villages that would have to be abandoned. Then they would chalk out a programme for the day, the route they would take in the battered Land Rover from village to village. When it was finished they would look at each other, smile, and throw it away: they knew by now that at the first stop there would be a programme-buster, like someone who urgently needed some medicine they had not brought along. One of them would have to trudge back to pick it up, while the other followed news of injuries in an attack on some homestead which was never on the programme at all. Often they did not see each other again till they got back home in the evening.

Philomena had quickly come to recognise the severity of the work Carla did. In a matter of months her own body changed. The idle plumpness rapidly combusted, and all that was left were the useful bits of fibre and muscle and tissue. Her sinews began to stand out as her frame turned wiry. Her skin turned crinkly and weather-beaten. They worked tirelessly through famines and assaults and battles. Stalking the fiery, never-ending landscapes day after day, trudging through the clammy claustrophobia of the afternoon deluges. Instructing, screaming, sometimes mending and winning, sometimes sadly surrendering. They rested little, ate even less. Here there was no spring, no winter. The seasons and their beauties were luxuries to be savoured in some other, gentler world. Here the years melded into each other in an endless molten flow of death, succour, celebration, and death again.

Now, several years on and only in her mid-forties, she looked at herself in the small mirror nestling in the thatched wall of the hut and saw that the colour of her hair was changing, her face slowly being framed in silver. The face itself had changed. It was stronger, more distilled. Perhaps there was a hint of achievement in the lines on it, but it was submerged beneath the tortured images she faced day after day in the villages and fields that were her offices. Their work was steeped in the sorrow of others, and every brisk walk away from the dying eyes of children was so crushing a defeat and the defeats poured in so rapidly, that there seemed something faintly obscene about feeling any sense of achievement. Yet somewhere inside her, for the first time in her life she felt... useful.

When she returned home in the evening, Philomena would occasionally be overwhelmed by it all. Sometimes she would sit and stare helplessly into the distance, like the children she had cradled gently to their deaths during the day, and sometimes she would just sit and weep. Most often she felt anaesthetised, numb and empty.

She could see now that Carla's deadpan demeanour, her often brutal flippancy, were really only the bandages that covered up the horrors she had known and felt deeply about. It was easier easy to push the images away till they merely became distant flashes from a somehow unrelated world. It was the easy way out, and Philomena was determined to not take it. For hours she would fight the jumbled images of maggoty intestines, suppurating limbs and torn innards that they had cauterised and gently, hopelessly replaced in bodies, bodies with eyes that stared hopefully at them with gratitude and trust that they both knew was misplaced.

Over those years, Nestor's work took him further and further away for longer and longer. But the more obscure his movements, the longer his absences, the more

Philomena grew to love him. She never asked him where he had been or why he had gone, and she was happy when he sometimes told her of his own volition. She knew he spoke to Milton for hours about these things, and she was surprised that Milton was willing to show any interest in the details of Nestor's escapades and of the movement. She found herself mildly irritated by Nestor's ability to speak freely to Milton about a part of his life that Milton so violently disapproved of, but perhaps Nestor needed him to just listen, and she did not question his choices.

Their moments together were gusts of bliss snatched from the winds, the rarer the lovelier. Sometimes they would lie together listening to the staccato pattering of the warm afternoon rain on the earthen water drum outside, then revel in the shining, sun-drenched landscape afterwards. They played on Akimbo's Head with Christopher, and Nestor would always end up giving in to the boy's persistent demands that Nestor tell him what he called 'war stories'. They would sit there together and Nestor would relate stories of the revolution while Christopher stared out wide-eyed over the rippling plains at imaginary battlefields.

Sometimes she would sit and watch as Nestor and Milton and the boys played the game of football with the other kids. She watched as the games became tougher. She began to notice how Christopher was becoming harder and stronger, whether he was flying into a tackle or holding off an opposition player. She watched as he absorbed injuries, thinking nothing of picking himself up and playing on with the gashed thigh or a cut forehead.

One evening Christopher trudged into the hut, and sat heavily on his bed.

'Look at you! You're filthy! Get off the bed. Is that blood?' She asked, pointing at his arm.

Christopher looked at his arm in surprise. He wiped the blood off, grinning. 'Yep. But not mine. Is there anything to eat?

Philomena stared at him, then smiled.

'What?' asked Christopher.

'Your voice. It's broken. It's a man's voice.'

Christopher smiled sheepishly. 'It's been happening a while. I am almost sixteen now, mum.'

'You're fifteen, young man,' said Philomena firmly. Christopher laughed. 'Okay, if it makes you feel younger.'

'Cheeky bugger,' she muttered.

Philomena gazed at Christopher. 'So, what are you going to do with your life? Any ideas?'

Christopher gazed steadily back. 'University. Politics and philosophy,' he said.

'Hmm,' said Philomena, getting up. She put some *tizet* and golden eggs on a plate and handed it to Christopher. She watched him eat, reconciling herself to the fact that she would soon lose her son to the world.

A few months on, in late December when the rain had just begun to carry the hint of a chill, a realisation flashed in Philomena that Nestor too had aged. One evening, Nestor had seemed more distracted than she had ever seen him before. When she asked him about it he had stared through her as if she wasn't there at all. Looking at him, she had seen for the first time what an elderly Nestor would look like.

As he gazed through Philomena, Nestor was in turmoil within. It had been troubling him for some while now, and he had finally been forced to accept that there was no other logical answer: There was an informer amongst them.

The operation he had headed some months ago had been a simple one. They were to eliminate a village headman who had been supplying his village's crop to the army. Stealing silently into the long grass on the edge of the clearing where the headman's hut stood, they had watched as a couple of men stood conversing with the headman in the doorway of the hut. A woman who had been sweeping outside the hut disappeared indoors and emerged a few minutes later. The men said their farewells and left with the woman. As the day grew gloomy with the afternoon sulk of the rain clouds, Nestor decided to move.

Signalling to the others to stay where they were, he slid forward, ruffling the still grass in his wake. Then he was out and striding across the clearing – stealth was of no value in the open. He strode into the hut, weapon in hand. The headman hadn't heard him enter. He was kneeling by a rough cot, talking softly to a baby within. Nestor levelled his gun and shot him twice in the back. The headman screamed and twisted round before crumpling to the floor in a groaning heap. Nestor took careful aim and shot him through the left eye. He stood a moment or two over the still body. The baby stared wide-eyed at him as he turned to leave. He walked briskly out of the hut.

Once outside, he broke into a half-run towards the high grass. Anxious faces poked out from some of the huts in the distance. He turned around and waved his gun at them, walking backwards. The faces retracted tortoise-like into the shadows.

But it was the subsidiary mission that required them to disable a minor communications post on their way back that had caused the trouble. Watching the post from the cover of the grass everything seemed normal. It had started to rain, and they could hear the dull rattle of the water beating down on the tin roofs of the communications cabin and the living quarters of the soldiers who manned the post. Two soldiers lounged about in the covered area in front of their quarters, chatting and singing. The door to the cabin, out of the line of sight of the soldiers, stood ajar.

Nestor and his men snaked forward towards the cabin, reassured by the continued singing of the soldiers. Lying flat on the floor, Nestor had pushed the door open slowly with the barrel of his gun. The cabin was unoccupied. There was an eruption of laughter from the direction of the soldiers quarters. Reassured, Nestor quickly entered the hut. It was empty, devoid of any equipment at all. Disconnected wires hung mockingly in mid-air. Nestor froze, then dropped to the floor. He crawled frantically out of the hut.

'Trap!' he hissed to the others.

He lifted his head and looked around slowly. He thought he saw the glint of metal amongst the grass in the distance. Out of the corner of his eye he saw another glint in the foliage. The soldiers continued to sing in their barracks, the music sounding like a taunt.

The others looked expectantly at Nestor. He held up his fingers in front of his face, counting them down from five. When the last one dropped they rose together and scattered, charging away in different directions. The gleaming metal in the bushes spat venomously at them. Nestor rolled and zigzagged to the high grass. The man closest to him seemed to exclaim with surprise, then thud to the ground. Lucky man, thought Nestor: the lucky ones were the ones who did not have time to start hoping before they died. Nestor kept going through the grass till he was reasonably sure that by some stroke of luck he had passed through a breach in the ambushers' lines. Breathing heavily, he smiled: in the circumstances, they must have been supremely incompetent to have failed to wipe out the whole unit.

The soldiers in the distance seemed to now be spraying the grass with random fire. Suddenly from quite close by he heard one of his men whisper his name. Signalling him to fall back further, he began a crouching retreat himself, checking and cross-checking that they were not being followed.

When they converged later, Nestor strode along in silence. His colleague noticed the concentrated ferocity in Nestor's eyes and the fury in his walk. They climbed up to a ridge and dropped down over the other side onto a path that led to a safe village they had all used from time to time. Gradually, their pace slackened. As they walked the path, Nestor's rage finally took voice.

'Who was the runner who brought the orders for the radio post?' he asked. His eyes were cold as he stared straight ahead.

'I don't know – it was some *naada*,' said his colleague, who Nestor knew to be from a rival tribe.

Nestor stopped dead in his tracks. He turned to the man and dealt him a lashing blow to his face. '*naada*, devil, angel, who cares?' he roared. 'Names, what was his name? If you don't know, don't speak!'

The man mumbled a name.

'Detain him the next time he delivers a message.'

Nestor called for an urgent meeting of the council. Three days later the suspect runner was detained. He was carrying instructions for a mission which passed off without incident. The man was released. He carried again, and though everyone was a little more wary when they went out on the assignments he had carried to them, it soon became apparent that he was not the leak. Then one day it was settled irrevocably: the runner was found lying in the bramble with his throat slit neatly open, his meagre possessions untouched.

The killings continued, with no discernible common link. Runners, rebels, even their families, were cut down with terrifying precision. They changed the routes of the runners and a few weeks later the ambushes started on the new routes. Missions were undertaken in the strictest secrecy, the men only informed of the target when they were actually on their way. But the traps continued unabated. Every meeting of the council was tense, clouded over by the treachery afoot. An idea had slowly been creeping into the heads of the members. It remained unspoken, but there was a grating tension in the air.

Finally one day the Hook gave voice to what they all already knew. In a low, grave voice he said: 'That leaves only us. It is one of us.'

The walls of distrust that had slowly been building were suddenly complete. Nestor could see the others' minds working as his worked too; reviewing past incidents, things they had said, motives for betrayal, opportunities for cover-ups. It seemed that any of them could be the one, but clearly it was Nestor who had escaped most often. So often and so uncannily that it was obvious that the analysis of the others would lead them to zero in upon him. A sinister new factor had been introduced into the already dangerous world they operated in.

# Twenty-four

'Solid hot, *yaar*!' said Ghanshyam Batak, junior partner of Sweety Constructions, running a sodden handkerchief ineffectually over his face. He made a low gargling sound and ejected a thick stream of *paan*-laden spittle onto the gatepost of the Casa de Familia DaCruz. 'And this is supposed to be the monsoon!'

He cast a critical eye over the rambling house at the end of the driveway. 'Area?' he asked in a bored manner.

'One, one half acre.'

'That much?' Batak looked at the house with renewed greed. 'Problems are there, no? That stupid Parsi woman we met is not the owner, isn't it? Title-holder is in Singaapoor or Hong Kong or something, no?'

'His wife was here for some time, but she passed away last year,' volunteered the sidekick.

'Mmm... the power of attorney that woman showed us includes sale?'

'No, sir.'

'Mmm...' Batak scratched his cheek reflectively, leaving dry streaks on the sweating oily skin. 'Mmm... okay, we will convince her it does. Come on, let us inspect.'

They picked their way through the bramble, taking measurements, calculating gradients, analysing the relief. When they had finished, Batak's crisp white safari suit (regulation apparel for the successful and deceitful Indian businessman) was decidedly off colour. His white patent leather shoes, that other shining manifestation of twisted success, were scratched and muddied.

'*Satyanash*!' he exclaimed, looking down at them. 'I will have to buy new ones, and the missus will do *bak-bak* for days!' He looked up at the house. 'Come on, let us go in. You have the keys, no?'

The sidekick hesitated. 'People say there is danger inside,' he said nervously.

Batak frowned in exasperation and a large drop of sweat seized the opportunity to roll down a furrow on his forehead and deposit itself in his eye. He swore loudly and wiped his eye. 'Ghosts, no? All rub-bish. Give me the keys, idyut! If your cousin had not been the Collector I would have sacked you long ago!' He snatched the keys and strode off towards the house on his own.

As he mounted the steps to the veranda, a cloud that seemed to have been marking time over the sea rolled in, obscuring the sun. Batak noticed the change and cursed silently. 'It couldn't have come while we were surveying outside, huh?' he muttered to himself.

197

The sidekick looked up apprehensively at the sky. He noticed the light over the house had changed. The blazing sunlight that had exorcised the wild jumble in the garden had given way to some bleaker force. The bramble seemed to throw out sharp, evil-looking claws for the grey wind to sharpen. He moved backwards towards the gate. All at once the rain came. Angry clouds of spray exploded off the undergrowth and drifted towards the house, following the pointing fingers of the hissing branches.

Batak jiggled the ancient iron key around in its slot. It refused to turn. His efforts increased in their violence, and finally a brutal jerk-and-twist combination did the trick. The hinges howled as the door reluctantly opened. A projecting splinter of wood gouged Batak's hand. He shrieked and kicked the door in fury. Sucking on the wound, he entered the Casa de Familia DaCruz. His sidekick waited for him to disappear before spinning around and scurrying off down the road.

Batak pulled out a pencil torch from his trouser pocket and switched it on. Out of the darkness, glaring straight at him, were a pair of malevolent eyes. He cried out loud, and the mongoose he had disturbed jumped off the table and scurried away. Batak sucked in a deep breath of dank air.

He swung the torch around. There were cobwebs everywhere. Batak felt as if he was at the centre of some colossal web, and the spider was watching, waiting. As he moved about, the webs that spanned the dark, silent spaces between the furniture slipped their silken shackles around his legs.

He walked through a huge, dark room into a smaller, even darker room, with doors leading off on either side. The entrance was now far behind, its grey light too feeble to reach him now. The latches on the doors he opened screeched in protest before succumbing with a crack that bounced off the walls and swooped around the still house.

The door to the left led to what must have been the kitchen, another still and silent room. He turned and crossed over to the door on the right. Crack. Push. It wouldn't give. Batak heaved. The door screamed and groaned, then keeled over into the room beyond.

It was a small room with windows on either side which had been boarded up like all the others. But there was a single crack in the boards on each of the windows, through which a dull light trickled. Catching the dust that the falling door had stirred up, it created two giant blue sheets that streamed across from either side of the room and converged at Batak's feet. As he looked down in front of him, they appeared to form a cross on the floor. He crossed his arms over his chest and noticed that though the air inside the house was cool, he was perspiring again. He stepped backwards away from the room swinging his flashlight over the brooding walls, trying to dispel the heavy menace the house was now oozing.

He re-entered the large central room he had passed, still moving backwards, not turning around for fear of what he might face or what he might fatally have turned his back upon. Then something pressed up against his back, cutting off his retreat.

Petrified he whirled around, his torch clattering to the floor. Snatching it up with trembling hands, he trained it on his tormentor. It was an ornate high-backed armchair with its back to him. Batak was sure it had not been there earlier.

Shaking with fear, Batak clattered backwards in the dark towards the entrance, sweeping his torch around wildly. It caught the deep, high ceiling, and he froze. Three ceiling fans with upturned blades hung in a row from the rafters. And they were on.

Batak whimpered. The fans swirled around faster and faster, whipping up an inferno of dust and danger. Batak gazed transfixed at the three gyrating monsters as they showered their malevolence upon him. He somehow tore his eyes away and stumbled towards the distant door, struggling in the teeth of a sudden, howling wind that was flying in through it. He stumbled over unseen tables and stools, finally crawling out sobbing into the sombre grey-black monsoon light.

Batak turned to slam the door closed and shut away the evil within. There, framed by the far door of the accursed dark hall, were two white lights, shining from the eyes of a gigantic man wearing a fisherman's *lungi*. Perhaps it was his eyes, perhaps only his rampant imagination, but as Batak stood riveted, staring at the wild mane of hair that framed the eyes and the translucent golden torso, he could swear he saw a great maniacal grin break out under the burning eyes. The giant seemed to lift his fists in triumph. Then he threw his head back into the shadows and let out a great roar that drowned out the thunder form the heavens.

Batak fled down the driveway, shrieking for his assistant. When he did not appear, Batak continued without stopping down the road till the sights and sounds of normality calmed him – a paan-wallah clinking his mallet on a brass bowl, a dog serenely chewing on a piece of dried fish. He slowed down and looked around, spotting his sidekick lounging idly about at a tea stall. He slowed down his step to a brisk strut.

They walked back towards the house together. In the guise of showing his assistant a beam of structural importance on the veranda, he casually asked him to lock the front door while he pretended to study other aspects of the house.

On the way back to the office his sidekick smiled and asked what sir thought of the place.

'No...' said Batak in a grave voice. 'Too many legal problems. We can manage the power of attorney, of course, but we are not that type of people.'

# Twenty-five

As time had moved on from this time to the next and the time beyond, Philomena had abandoned the detail of it. She did not remember the date or month or year of famines or upheavals or births or funerals – such benchmarks seemed petty in the face of the sweep of life. There was a date on the lone letter she received from Edson, now settled in Hong Kong, and for a few moments she had wrestled with how long it had taken to reach the bus stop for Carla to pick up. One and a half months, she noted placidly. It was the same with the letter from her mother, who had returned to the Casa de Familia DaCruz in 1985, finally unable to live with the distance Edson had sought to put between them and where they belonged.

Every night Philomena would sit in the glow of the lamp, sometimes with Nestor, often alone, and later with Christopher at her side, listening to the BBC telling of this and that. She sat with Christopher and listened to John Peel and Tommy Vance, trying to shape Christopher's musical consciousness into her own. She had listened to the reports of the repression unleashed by India's new Gandhi. Later, when elections had been announced, Philomena had made a mental note of the date of the elections and for those brief days had pegged her thoughts to dates and months, only to discard such technicalities when the event was over. And much later, when communism finally relented, she again absorbed the fact and discarded the time and date.

Alamai's message of death too had also been absorbed without reference to month or year. It had happened; irretrievably and finally, and the details were irrelevant.

*

Philomena had been strolling about the village looking for fuel for the lamp and Christopher, in that order. Carla had just returned from one of her periodic bus-stop trips. She had called Philomena over and handed her the letter.

The stamp on it had been defaced in Bombay on '13.8.94'. She glanced at Carla's wall calendar. A month and a half again, she thought as she looked at the unfamiliar handwriting. She had torn it open and seen the childish, laboured hand of Alamai.

'Dear Philomena,

This is to inform you that dear Tehmina passed away peacefully on 10th August from kidney failure at the

Parsi General Hospital. She had been suffering from kidney problems for a long time and was in serious pain for the last three weeks. She did not want to bother you. I would have informed you anyway but I did not know how. Lancelot I had informed, and he was to come, but yesterday he telephoned to say that it is now pointless for him to come. Your address I have somehow got from your father. He has not come because it was your mother's wish to be lain to rest in the Towers of Silence and he informed me that he would not go there ever again. He said that the only reason he went there was because dear Tehmina wanted him to, and now the reason was gone. We will all live in the shadow of this great loss.

After Dara passed away I had no one here except your mother. Now I am alone. Binaifer came down from Canada last month to help me shift to the Parsi sanatorium at Bandra. Do you remember it? On the sea at Bullock Road? It is not like having your own home, but Binny says it will be more convenient here. Please write to me. I will enjoy hearing from you. No one gets any letters here, but the sea is beautiful, and it never goes away like people do.

The address is...'

Philomena walked quietly over to the window at the back of Carla's hut. The warm evening wind ruffled the wide African grasslands. She shuddered as she gazed out over the enormous, rippling landscape that she had come to know so well. An image jumped into her mind. Firecrackers and ship's silhouettes on the Arabian Sea, punched black designs of wrought iron railings. A wave of loneliness washed over her. She shivered again and crossed her arms across her chest, shielding herself from this vast and suddenly alien place spread out in front of her. She stood there for a long time, her mind wandering over to her parents and Arun and Jesus and Kenkre and all the others she had toyed with in the happy rush of youth.

Realising where Philomena was and that there was something in the letter that had taken her there, Carla slipped quietly out of the house.

Alone in the faltering light of dusk, Philomena finally found the reason for the despair that had enveloped her. She really could not remember making one single gesture – a pat on the arm, a smile that her mother could have taken to mean she loved her. It had never struck her as being necessary – her mother was always going to be there, there was always later. And anyway it was understood, it needed no manifestation.

She sank slowly to her haunches by the window. A low, strangled sound rose from within her, gnarled and twisted with regret, and then she began to sob. She cried not as one cries for departed lovers or broken dreams but with the deep, bitter despair of redemption irretrievably forgone.

Later, as they walked back home, Christopher had wondered why his mother was holding onto his arm quite so tightly.

*

When at home, Nestor was sullen and short at precisely the time that Philomena needed to know most that there was something or someone that kept her there, that needed her presence. Unseeing and oppressed himself, Nestor pushed her away. She tried to tell him of her insecurity, but something always made her stop short of an honest confession. In her desperation, she pushed back the borders that pride had drawn in around her, even knocked down little bits of the walls of indifference she had so blithely traded in for so long. Nestor did not notice. She felt his indifference, his contempt for the triviality of her concerns. He would cut her off mid-sentence with a dismissive wave of his hand or a question which made it clear that he had not been listening, and she would smile and shrug away the slight. Some days she would tell him of the horrors Carla and she had faced, and he would smile patronisingly, like Philomena herself had many years ago when a visitor to Bombay had told her how difficult life was in the west if you weren't wealthy.

She nurtured her bitterness, feasted on the injustice of it all. She had given up other lives to live this one with him. *He* was who she was here for. *They* had a child; a child whom Nestor only seemed to see as the biological successor to his cause. She began to neglect her work, making excuses she knew Carla knew were untrue. Half-knowing he wouldn't understand yet, she tried to talk to Christopher about things she could not ever bring herself to mention to someone who would understand: love, regret, loss, lost love, love that bred regret. She realised with despair that her son was already beginning to hide himself away from her. She could see the awkwardness growing in him when she spoke about her feelings. And when she looked into his eyes she saw the fledgling sparks of the same fire that subsumed Nestor. Her mind wandered back to what Carla had told her the evening they had arrived.

One day she asked Kanu about Carla. Carla, who had changed the way the village looked at itself: made it feel a little bigger, a little more important, a little more part of the world outside. Kanu confessed to knowing very little about her other than the fact that she had considered the village to be her place for as long as he could remember and had never returned to her home outside Frankfurt even for a visit, and that there were rumours of a widow in a neighbouring village being her lover.

As he spoke Carla herself appeared, striding towards them. Philomena surprised herself by noticing for the first time the easy freedom with which Carla breasts moved beneath her fatigues. As she drew closer, Philomena saw dark clouds scudding across Carla's face. She thrust a printed piece of paper roughly at Philomena.

'Here! The whole place is flooded with them. The latest attempt at legalised theft. A Happiness Tax!' she snorted and stomped off.

Kanu took the paper from Philomena. He unfolded it carefully and peered at it. Philomena smiled and gently took it back from him. Turning it the right way up, she read:

## 'THE PROGRESSIVE NATIONALIST COUNCIL-IN-GOVERNMENT

### Resolution No. A/64-4382/HTX-Res.115/15It.

**WHEREAS** it is observed that it is in the interests of the citizens of the Republic, and whereas it is further observed that it is universally accepted practice that appropriate portions of the money earned by citizens are rendered as taxes to the government, and whereas it is also accepted universal practice that the accumulation of wealth and the consequential happiness therefrom requires and carries with it the obligation to contribute appropriate portions to government as and by way of taxes, the Council-in-Government has at its 35th Assembly tabled, discussed, ratified and promulgated 'The Happiness (and Occasions of Happiness) Tax Act, 1996'.

Certain salient features of the Act are extracted hereunder. The extracts below are not exhaustive or verbatim and reference must be made to the Act itself for an exact determination of liability.

1. Marriage  (i)  1000 Gundas payable by each of the two immediate participatory families.

            (ii) A 500 Gunda omnibus tax by each of the two immediate participatory families in lieu of separate collections from the extended immediate families (uncles, aunts, etc.)

3. Births      (i)   750 Gundas for each male child
                           (ii)   500 Gundas for each female
                                   child

4. Birthdays      100 Gundas per citizen, payable on or before the 31st of January every year.

(Provisions for refunds in the event of death prior to birthday are set out in Appendix XIX to the Act and such refunds will only be entertained upon appropriate applications being made at the Central Secretariat in the capital between 2 pm and 4 pm on the third Friday of each month).

5. Anniversaries   For the purposes of simplification of implementation, 50 Gundas will be payable by every citizen aged 15 years and over in lieu of a separate anniversary tax.

6. Social Entertainment      All events providing for the entertainment of over nine persons shall attract a tax of 50 Gundas. (Refunds, upon proof of cancellation of such event will be made as per Appendix XX to the Act and such refunds will only be entertained at the Central Secretariat in the capital between 2 pm and 4 pm on the third Friday of each month.)

| 7. Travel | 500 Gundas per person on all unofficial travel beyond 20 kilometres from known place of residence. |

| 8. Public Holidays | 2 Gundas per person per notified holiday. |

| 9. Health | 50 Gundas per person spending a period of less than three weeks in a calendar year in an accredited government hospital. |

| 10. Cultural & Religious | 25 Gundas per person for the attendance of any artistic, cinematic, dramatic, or other cultural performance. |

(For the purposes of this provision, an irrevocable presumption of happiness will be made regardless of any subsequent dissatisfaction with such performance. This provision includes village fayres, religious celebrations and feasts.)

(B) All payments are to be made at the jurisdictional police station unless otherwise specified.

(C) The Act shall come into effect from the 1st of January, 1997.

(D) In recognition of the sacrifice of personal happiness made by the members of the council in the execution of their duties, the members of the council and such persons as they may from time to time at their discretion designate shall stand exempted from the purview of the Act.

(E) For the purposes of simplification, an additional amount of 50 Gundas per person will be levied at the time of first payment in lieu of the taxes that are payable for the remaining months of 1996 (November and December).

(F) The penalties applicable for non-compliance with the provisions of the Act are set out in Appendix VI to the Act.

(F) Copies of the Act may be perused upon an application in the format to be published hereafter being made and approved by the Administrative Member, Council-in-Government.

Dated this 8th day of November, 1996'

Kanu finished counting on his fingers and looked up at Philomena with apprehension. His big, gentle eyes reflecting his confusion. 'I am that happy?'

\*

Not long after that the letter arrived. In an official-looking envelope marked to the name of Mr Christopher Musambe. Philomena carried it back up to the hut.

Nestor and Christopher were sitting outside and, by the looks of it, arguing. About politics as usual, thought Philomena.

'Letter for Mr Christopher Musambe,' she said, handing it over.

Nestor and Philomena watched as Christopher opened the letter and read.

'I have admission,' he said. 'Finally. I have admission. And a scholarship!'

His parents smiled at him. 'Super! Great news!' they said, each one feeling a little sick inside.

'When...' started Nestor.

'Bloody hell! It says I have to "...report to the University Registry by 10 am. on 31$^{st}$ September 1997." That's a week away! Why couldn't they have said earlier?'

'Because the letter is probably a month old,' said Philomena.

Christopher looked at it again. 'Next bus out then, I suppose. I'd better get cracking!'

Philomena rose abruptly and went outside. She had always known that this time would come, but somehow she was prepared for the suddenness of it, this brutal termination of her little crutch, and in a strange way, her... usefulness.

Sensing that Philomena was upset, Christopher had followed her out. He came up behind her and put an arm around her.

'It's all right, mum. I won't be disappearing entirely, you know.'

'I know,' said Philomena dully. 'It's just... you were always the anchor, Chris. Without you... I tried...'

'You've been fantastic, mum. Really. Everything I know, all that I read, heard, all from you. From dad too, but mostly... so much from you. But I really need to do this now. You know that. You know you want me to.'

'Yes, of course,' she said.

Christopher squeezed her shoulder. 'I'll just go down and tell the others about it.'

She watched as her son loped away down the path. From the corner of her eye she could see that Nestor was standing at the door, watching her. She kept her head turned away from him so he wouldn't see her eyes glistening.

'He's a good boy,' said Nestor. 'You're lucky you didn't have to handle the callousness your parents got when you left.'

Philomena set her lips and continued to stare into the distance. Then she walked away down the path without a word.

# Twenty-six

Nestor grew more distracted and withdrawn as the treachery continued. And then there was this new outrage, this 'Happiness Tax'.

The previous month they had lost Bene, cut down in an ambush too clinical and precise to have claimed a council member merely by coincidence. The members of the council deliberately operated in random and erratic ways, their movements impossible to predict. The mission that Bene had been on had been too outrageous for the military to have ever anticipated. They had known. Someone had given them the information.

Now there were only three of them. Instead of closing ranks, the atmosphere had turned sour and suspicious. Nestor wondered in private as to why the Hook always managed to somehow avoid the more dangerous operations of late. He had overheard Solomon muttering to the Hook how it was strange that Nestor had been the only survivor in so many savage encounters.

Months turned into a year, and then beyond. The killings continued. Runners, informers, suppliers, all began to disappear or turn up dead. Nestor grew gloomier.

'It is getting to you, you know, this intrigue,' said Milton one evening as Nestor finished telling him of the latest problems the rebels were facing. 'Just look at you! Old and grey, battle-beaten.'

Nestor grinned. 'I am surrounded by greying people,' he said, pointedly staring at Milton's own hair. 'At least I have an excuse for greying! Maybe Phil has too. What is yours? Worrying about the crop?'

Milton smiled. 'Maybe one day you will see my worries too. Have you ever worried about the future, your son's future here? I have. Have you ever worried about Nestor Musambe's safety every time he is away? I have. Have you ever tried to be indifferent to what is happening around us, ever turned away and tried to shut it out? Have you any idea at all what it is like to barter your soul away and convince yourself that it is best that way?'

They fell silent, till Milton sighed and asked dully, 'So when are you leaving again for the council meeting?'

'Day after.'

On a bright December morning, Philomena strolled over to Milton's field. Nestor had not returned from his latest foray. She watched Milton harvesting millet with Titi. Milton said something to his son, and Titi's reply made him laugh aloud. She noticed the sinewy bulges on

Titi's thighs as he worked. The man had pushed through some time back, but Titi rested content to work the fields of his father.

She called out to Milton, and after a bit he came over to where she sat in the shade of a bush and let himself down beside her. She said nothing. Milton stared at her quizzically, then turned his gaze away, shaking his head slowly.

'How did you pass so quickly from youth to this weary woman I see before me?' he asked softly.

Philomena smiled wryly. 'Maybe I lived twice as fast.'

Milton continued as if he hadn't heard her. 'These years, they should be years of anchorage, a safe harbour found, moorings being tightened. And here you are in the middle of all this... madness. And yet there is contentment to be found here too, but it only comes from the struggle to build something. There is no happiness to be found in destruction, no matter how evil the things you seek to destroy may be. The older you get the less the overlap between excitement and happiness. You came here chasing the one and find yourself craving the other, and you still cannot accept what you already know to be true – that Nestor is not and will never be yours to be happy with.'

Philomena winced inside at the brutal words. 'So what do I do now, now that I have chosen so badly?' she asked. 'I have a father who sits in Hong Kong with any old Englishman who will talk to him, and I had a mother who lived and died trying to make her husband's choices her own. Oh yes, I almost forgot; I also have a brother who my father adores because he is in England, who could have called my father over to live with him and be happy but never did. And I had Nestor in some distant age. Now all I have is my son and the carnage I see around me when I go to work, and even Christopher has slipped away from me. What do I build with that?'

They fell silent again. Milton shifted uncomfortably, wondering whether to continue. Finally he said: 'We build nothing here. Nestor, Carla, the others you see here, they are all phantoms. They have never been fleshed out with happiness, made complete. Christopher has been running around with Nestor's guns mouthing slogans when he was five. You have taught him well, but what chance does he have to build anything good? Thank God he has left, but I fear his heroes are men of violence, his ideals moulded out of this sad, perverted clay we till and harvest and till again. And you sit there and respect Nestor's choices. This is not respect, it is negligence! What is it that stopped you from giving your son the normal happy things he should have had? Why didn't you tell him more often that Nestor's way is wrong, help him with his choices? Do you love Nestor too blindly to bother about your son and his future? Or is it just that you couldn't care less?'

Philomena was silent a long while. 'It was the easiest way to make my son love me too. And he does. It was one fight I couldn't bear to take on, that I was too scared I'd lose.'

Milton looked long at her. Then he stood up, sighing. 'Just ask yourself this: if Nestor died one day in this battle of his, would this place still be the same for you? Would you look upon us or even Christopher the way you do today? What really would be left for you here? Your answer will be the answer to the question you came here to ask but never did.'

As they rose to leave Milton noticed that Philomena's leg had frozen and helped her up. They walked towards the village.

As they neared, they noticed that there seemed to be some sort of commotion. A little girl saw them from a distance and ran towards them, shouting something about Nestor and that they should come quickly.

A crowd had gathered on the open path between the main cluster of huts and the rise to Nestor's hut. As they pushed their way through, they saw a motionless heap lying in the dust, the earth around it slushy with gore and blood. Nestor's face was caked with bloody dust. His body suddenly heaved, drawing in huge gulps of air. Carla was bent over him, methodically cutting away a trouser-leg stiff from congealed blood.

When she finally peeled it away there was a horrified groan from the crowd. Knee down, you could recognise a leg. Above that a mass of flesh slopped flaccidly out of the trouser leg as the cloth came away. Carla appraised the mess before her critically. Without touching anything, she bent over and peered up and down the shambles. She pulled herself up, pronounced that the leg looked much worse than it was, and that Nestor should be carried to her hut.

The onlookers recoiled at the suggestion. Carla snapped out five names, pointing decisively at the men at she did so. The chosen ones moved forward reluctantly.

As they walked together, Carla glanced over at Philomena beside her.

'Flesh wound?' asked Philomena.

'Probably. In fact, almost certainly. We will have to check the rest of him, though, and he has lost a lot of blood.'

'Infection?'

Carla smiled thinly. 'My my! It seems as if I'm going to get some decent assistance!' She shook her head in reply to the original question. 'Doesn't look like it, at least not yet. You never know with these things.'

Carla led them to the table in her room. She swept off the things that were lying on it and watched them lower Nestor onto the table, swearing at a slightly clumsy bearer. She roughly dismissed the chattering crowd that was looking in through the door and the windows. Milton sat in a corner and watched as the two women worked, admiring Carla's assured, methodical functioning and despairing at Philomena's detached assistance.

They cut away the rest of his clothes and cleaned up the gore, finding no further serious wounds. Then Carla went to work on the leg. Milton could now discern the punctures. Carla pointed at the bullet holes – two in, two out. They spoke softly about 'crater wounds', which Milton could gather were caused by a kind of bullet that ripped away the flesh at its point of entry.

As they splashed astringents and lotions on the raw red troughs, Nestor moved and groaned. Suddenly his eyes bulged open, his eyeballs close to bursting. His body snapped upward in an arch and his head jerked backwards, the veins on his forehead and in his neck engorged with blood he was supposed to have lost. Carla and Philomena struggled to hold him down. Then suddenly he went limp. Unhindered now, they worked quickly for over an hour on the motionless Nestor.

When they had finished, they washed themselves and briefly discussed the course of treatment. Philomena sat down next to Milton and suddenly left with nothing to do, anxiety flooded over her face.

Carla strode to the door, where a few of the villagers still waited patiently, squatting on their haunches. She smiled at them and said: 'He is all right. Thank you for your help and concern. The show is over. Go home now.'

She came back in, rummaged about, and came up with a tumbler of wine. Sinking to the floor beside the others, she passed the tumbler to Milton and pronounced: 'Much ado about not very much. The hands are badly scratched – he's obviously crawled a long way. But they will mend quickly, and there is nothing that will not heal in time. No point trying to move him tonight, so you might as well make yourself comfortable. There is plenty of beer, and I'll see what we can put together to eat.'

They ate from the small stock of tins which Carla didn't often touch, preferring the local *fufu* and soup or stew. Much later that night they drowsed uncomfortably, overcome with exhaustion and the effort of talking in the low, weighty tones that people adopt at times of crisis.

Suddenly Nestor groaned. 'Why not him?' he mumbled, softly but clearly through the dark. 'Why not him?' His voice was stronger this time.

They rushed over to where Nestor was lying.

'Why not him?' he repeated, over and over again.

Carla looked him over by the light of a candle, checking his bandages, looking to see that everything was in place. Drawing herself up, she said: 'It's all right. He is rambling. There is a slight fever.'

Nestor's eyes opened slowly. He cast them around, confused. His eyes slowly dropped back into focus and he smiled. 'So I made it back,' he said.

Looking down at himself he saw the huge crisp bandages on his body. 'Bad?'

'No,' replied Carla.

Her answer seemed to strengthen Nestor enough to remind him that he was thirsty. He managed to raise his head and drink with little support. Then he sank back again with a sigh and closed his eyes.

'Why not him?' he said it lucidly this time, emphasising each word.

'Why not who?' asked Milton gently, but Nestor had already drifted off to sleep again.

He woke frequently that night, and the night after but fell asleep again almost immediately. Towards morning on the third day he awoke properly for the first time and gradually began to talk coherently.

It was Milton who finally asked him some days later what had happened.

'We were going... We had a meeting after I left here – the council, I mean – to discuss the usual things...and this new tax the government has announced. But before we could start The Hook told us that his house had been torched the night before. At first he had dismissed it as an innocent accident: a spark on dry straw, a broken lantern, something like that. But he had looked around later and found a half-empty can of fuel abandoned in a bush nearby. His youngest daughter had been badly burned and had died in the morning. They were staring at me accusingly. I would have walked out forever there and then, but I had to stay to prove that they were wrong. As we left, we embraced the Hook one by one, and I could feel the emptiness within him.

'We left in the usual way, everyone in different directions. Solomon and I decided to walk some distance together before parting ways. I remember Solomon wanted to make a detour along the way to speak to a man about some straw he needed for his house. It meant going a fair way off the shortest route, and I suspected he did not want to walk with me on the obvious route. Or could it be that he was the informer and I was the one who was being set up? I agreed to go with him, but I was frightened and tense, and Solomon noticed this and became tense himself.

'We reached a faint path in the grass near the abandoned tin mine – you know the place, Milton. All at once, from within the whispering grass, I heard a rustle. Solomon heard it too. It could have been anything: an animal, someone cutting grass, a gust of wind. But somehow we both knew that the rustle we had heard was malignant. We glanced at each other and walked on, our eyes flicking around and at each other.

'Then the rustles began to come at us from different directions. They were all around us. As one, we reached for our weapons. The soldiers rose from the grass, surrounding us. A young boy, no more than fifteen, let off a blast from his gun. I felt the bullet hit my leg. As I began to fall over Solomon quickly ducked under my armpit to support me. I noticed that he looked at me differently, as though apologising for his suspicion. I pushed him away, screaming at him to run. He looked at me for a split second, remorse in his eyes, then dropped down and crawled into the grass.'

'The soldiers converged upon me. The leader was ranking... I can't remember... a captain at least. He strode past me to the spot where Solomon had disappeared and ploughed into the grass. Silence. Then pistol shots. Two, three, four, I can't remember.'

Nestor paused and gestured to Philomena. She brought him a glass of ginger drink, and he drank it down.

'You should rest,' said Philomena.

'You are certain they got Solomon?' asked Milton

Nestor looked into the distance. 'Oh yes. They got him. The soldiers closed the circle around me. One of them, a tall, thin man with a beautiful face and cold eyes, walked around and stood in front of me. Machete in one hand, he slowly he raised the gun in the other. He was wearing the most beautiful scarf I have ever seen. I prayed that he would not toy with me, that he would not blow away my groin, or slit open my bowels for me to watch, or any of the other things I had seen done before to others. His arm kept rising, and when he levelled the gun at my head I think I smiled with relief. I stared at the scarf, waiting for the snap of his pistol and wondering how much of it I would hear. Suddenly from behind me a voice barked out, "No! Not him."

223

'The officer who followed Solomon into the bush had returned. The other soldiers turned to him, puzzled. He glared them down. With an authoritative sweep of his hand he called them away.'

'So that's what you were rambling about,' said Philomena.

'Yes. Why not me?'

'Maybe they thought you were just Solomon's foot soldier,' said Milton.

'When did they start sparing foot soldiers?' asked Nestor. 'Anyway, I tested the wound. There didn't seem to be anything seriously wrong. I started out along the path and for a while I made good progress. I even thought I would be able to get back home before night came. But then I suddenly felt my strength go completely. I looked down and saw the blood. Bubbling over the brim of my body every time I took a step. Something went out of me, and I knew I had no chance of getting back that night.'

Nestor gestured to Philomena to help him sit up in the cot.

'You spent the night out in the open with the wound?' asked Milton incredulously.

Nestor saw Philomena's questioning look. 'You see, a wounded bleeding animal does not survive long at night in these parts. No, I struggled up a baobab tree standing on its own in the bush and found a broad branch to spend the night on. I could almost see the scent of blood spreading in the air. I shivered, waiting for the hyenas and leopards to arrive.'

Nestor closed his eyes and went silent. Philomena went over to him and felt his brow. His eyes remained shut.

Milton stood up. 'Let him sleep,' he said.

'I did not sleep that night,' said Nestor, his eyes still shut. 'I remember trying to stop the blood from running down the tree trunk. Most of all, I remember the... silence.'

He fell silent again, but as Milton turned to leave Nestor opened his eyes suddenly.

'I must have lost consciousness, I think, because when I came round the sun was high and the insects were feasting on my leg. I looked around. The world spun dizzily and I just dropped off the tree. The pain as I hit the ground was... After a couple of attempts at standing I decided to crawl. I had no idea how far I went that way. Nose in the dust, reach, anchor, drag, reach again. Again and again. And again. Hour after hour, on and on... At first the effort took everything. Then when I settled into the pattern, my mind began to work. Reach, anchor, drag... why not him? Reach, anchor... why not him? Drag... It kept coming back to me, what the soldier had said. Suddenly, I felt my strength drain away entirely and realised that I had been crawling uphill. I put my head down to rest, and that is the last thing I remember.'

Philomena had listened patiently, waiting, hoping for a mention of her, that she had been somewhere in his thoughts in those lonely hours. Now she turned away, disappointed.

Milton collected Nestor's tattered clothes from Carla's shed and took them to Nestor.

'I'm afraid they're useless,' he said. I found this in the pockets,' he said, handing over some coins and held up a soiled piece of paper. Nestor motioned Milton to put them down beside him.

Philomena glanced at the paper. It was a copy of the Happiness Tax notification.

Milton held up the paper. 'Why do you still carry this around?' he asked.

'To remind me. When I'm weak. Time dulls the horrors of a crime. So I pull it out and read it when I need to remember.'

Milton leaned over and patted Nestor's arm. 'I have to go now.'

'Stay a while, my friend,' said Nestor.

Milton shook his head. 'It's Sunday, Nestor. I must change the flowers on Clara's grave. It is a long way, and I'd like to be back before dark. I'll look in when I return.'

# Twenty-seven

As the months went by, Nestor recovered his strength with a swiftness that was surprising for a man his age. Left with nothing to do other than rest and hobble around, he seemed to be sucked deeper and deeper into the mystery of his reprieve. Sooner or later he would have to face the Hook. Sooner or later he would have to explain how he had managed to escape. He pondered long as to whether he should recount what had happened truthfully, say that he had been inexplicably spared when utterly defenceless. Would anyone still believe he was innocent? The penalty for betrayal was brutal and final, the standard of proof rough and ready. He himself had executed men on more slender grounds. He wondered whether it was proper for him in the interest of the greater truth to lie. Even if he did, the distrust would be thicker than ever. And yet, it was now beyond doubt that there was an informer. Solomon and he had been ambushed. After meeting at a place no one should have known of. Not on the regular path they would have taken home, but on an obscure detour that had only been mentioned casually at the meeting itself. With Solomon gone, it could only have been the Hook or himself. So it had to be the Hook. Or had they simply been followed? And why not him? Was he being set up? And by whom? It had to be by the Hook. He wondered if he should speak to the central council about it. The Hook would also perhaps do the same, so should he speak to them before he told the Hook? There would be new faces elevated to the council soon. He ran through the probables in his head, trying to analyse their attitude towards him. And could one of *them* possibly be the one?

In the midst of all this turmoil Philomena tended to him, cared for him as she had never cared for anyone before. She stopped working altogether to be at home for him, and he found her constant presence vaguely irritating. She changed his bandages, plied him with special food, even helped him relieve himself. He saw her devotion as a kind of annoying servility. As he wrestled with his problems, she would interrupt with mundane inquiries about medicine and food. Then he began to snap at Philomena. Even more unexpectedly, the more he berated her the less she challenged him. The waters tested, the downward spiral that had started with his commitment to the rebel movement to the exclusion of all else rushed onward towards the final destruction of their relationship. When Philomena asked him about his troubles, he waved her away. When she silently complied, believing he was troubled and needed his space, her very silence fuelled his contempt.

On and on it went, till one day Nestor called her a gutless whore and was astonished when she smiled gently and said nothing. The descent was now complete – the scorn and abuse poured freely from him at every opportunity. He made fun of her in front of people, telling them how stupid and 'foreign' she was.

One night Milton sat beside Nestor's cot chatting. Nestor had mentioned the need to visit the toilet a little earlier. Philomena finished up whatever she was doing and went to help him up. Nestor continued talking and waved her away. Misunderstanding the wave, she bent over and grasped his arm. Something snapped in him. His face contorted with rage and he fisted her in her stomach. She yelled out in pain and backed away stunned. Without speaking, she turned and left. Nestor turned away to continue talking to Milton. Milton looked at him coldly, no longer listening. He stood up abruptly. 'So you are the men who hope to rule a better country,' he said softly.

Philomena sat outside till dawn. Nestor did not go to her.

She came in early the next morning and walked over to Nestor's bed. 'How could they ever mistrust you?' she said calmly. 'You would even kill me if I stood in the way of your grand cause.' Then she smiled coldly. 'I like what he is doing, this traitor of yours – finishing off your movement and sparing you.'

Nestor screwed up his face in distaste, but there was a hint of contrition mixed in somewhere.

Philomena continued to nurse him, and soon Nestor was able to walk around on his own, albeit slowly. They were silent days. Philomena refused to speak to him at all. Nestor tried once to talk to her about the problems facing him, but she walked out of the room mid-sentence and Nestor abandoned the effort forever.

Philomena was inexorably being driven nearer to a resolution, and before long she knew that she would take the decision she had been dreading.

# Twenty-eight

Nestor had in the meantime taken to walking over to Milton's hut every morning, from where they would walk down together to Milton's field.

It was the same that morning, except that when Nestor reached Milton's hut he found that Milton had already gone on ahead, leaving Titi behind. Nestor spotted the boy through the window. The chest in which Milton kept his memorabilia lay open. Letters, photographs, degrees, diaries lay strewn upon the floor. Nestor smiled and went in. He let himself down gingerly onto the floor beside Titi.

Together they pried into Milton's things. Nestor gazed wide-eyed at the profusion of envelopes with Indian stamps and familiar handwriting, surprised at the number of letters he had written to Milton while he had been away. He explained to Titi who the people on the stamps were. After a moment's hesitation, he read out letter after letter written by him to Milton, fleshing out names and places unknown to Titi. He smiled with embarrassment at an arrow he had drawn on a photograph of Philomena, on top of which he had written 'This is HER!', and laughed out loud at a picture of Philomena and the syndicate in front of Romeo. They rummaged about happily, Nestor reminiscing airily to his eager and receptive audience. He told Titi stories about Romeo and Kailash and the helicopters and they laughed uproariously. The chest was a treasure trove of memories that time had gilded with golden edges. Betrayal and trouble disappeared for a while. Time and again they dipped into the chest and came up with a fistful of stories. Many of the things in the box had to do with Milton's days at university involving people neither of them knew, and these they flung aside uninspected.

When the box was empty Nestor theatrically stuck a hand in and made a sad face, and they both laughed. Then they noticed that the chest had a false bottom. Grinning sheepishly, like errant schoolboys, they pulled the cover off. The papers within they removed more carefully in deference to their pride of place: Milton's bequest, legal titles to land, a photograph of his wife Clara. He glanced down at the remaining papers and froze.

In Milton's neat handwriting was a fading draft, heavily overscored with corrections: 'The Happiness (and Occasions of Happiness) Tax Act, 19...' Nestor picked it up, not so much reading but struggling with the realisation of what was before him.

Page after page. The entire Act. Drafted by Milton. He looked into the chest again and found blank government-issue expense slips and a small pocket diary. In it were notes of virtually everything Nestor had told Milton about the rebels, details of every incident, every plan, every proposal Nestor had ever spoken to Milton about.

'What is it?' asked Titi anxiously, noticing the rage that had swept over Nestor's face.

Nestor turned to the boy. 'Nothing,' he spat out viciously. Then he jumped up, grabbing his machete and stormed to the door.

Turning, he said, 'Milton has hurt me, Titi. He has hurt me.'

Titi rushed out behind Nestor. He grabbed hold of his arm. 'What is it? Tell me!'

Nestor shook off the boy without breaking his stride. Titi grabbed Nestor again. 'No, Nestor, no! You are wrong. He is a good man! He has tried to help you! He told me he has. Really, he did.'

Nestor pushed Titi roughly aside again. Titi stumbled and fell to the ground, but rose quickly to harry Nestor again. 'Stop! Please, stop!

Nestor strode on through the village, looking neither left nor right. Philomena poked her head out of Carla's window to see what the disturbance was about. Nestor walked past the house, his nostrils flared with rage as he fended Titi off again and again, each time more viciously. The boy's entreaties became wilder and more desperate, Nestor's patience grew shorter.

'My father is right, he has always done what is right!' The veins on Nestor's forehead throbbed dangerously.

Titi's frenzy reached a crescendo. 'My father says you

think you are brave, but you are weak! See, you can't even fight me! Stand and fight me!'

Nestor snarled with rage and flung Titi aside again. Titi came back at Nestor. 'You can't even fight me! Come on, stop and fight me first, old man! Loser! You are a loser!'

Nestor stopped dead in his tracks, his face crumpled with fury. He whirled around, his machete slashing the air as he turned and slicing clean through the boy's neck. The head came to rest in the dust, the tears bright and wet on the its face. Nestor turned away and resumed his march towards Milton's field.

As he neared the field Milton looked up towards him, smiling. 'What is all the commotion about?' he called out.

As Nestor neared, Milton noticed the look on Nestor's face, and his brow furrowed questioningly.

'Come,' said Nestor in a stranger's voice, raising his weapon an inch or two.

Milton noticed the splash of blood on the machete and the aggression in the gesture. The confusion on his face slipped away. He sighed and reached out to touch Nestor's arm. Nestor brushed him off and strode away ahead of Milton.

Before they reached the spot where Titi lay, Nestor pushed Milton into a gap between the huts that led out towards the open grasslands. He swept up a machete that someone had left leaning against the wall of one of the huts. He strode on, a hidden force guiding them, as always, to Akimbo's Head. Some of the villagers tried to follow them, but Nestor turned and raised the machete and they quickly scattered.

Nestor pushed Milton to the ground. Standing over him he whispered through his fury: 'Why?'

Milton picked himself up, a smile on his face. Sitting down heavily on a boulder, he said, 'I asked you the same question many years ago. You tell me first.'

Nestor raised his machete to Milton's face. 'Enough! No more bloody games. Why did you do this?'

Milton pushed the weapon away from his face. 'To save us. Long before you came back there was violence. Horrible violence. Pushes into the area, big pushes. Why do think they spared us? Why wasn't the village touched? Because of *me*. And maybe you too... The rebels always somehow felt you would return to fight for them. From here.'

'How did they know I would be a rebel? And what if I hadn't joined them?'

'I know you better than anyone else – I told them you would.'

'You... filth! And now you help these people. These swine who want to break us, destroy us?'

'All I know is that while you were playing Romeo in India, I saved a village. I saved lives.' He stared straight at Nestor. 'I saved lives,' he repeated slowly. 'What have you saved? Who have you saved? You can't even save your own life!'

'So why didn't you tell them about my movements? You knew most of them. They could have finished me off anywhere.'

'Oh, I did, but for different purposes. You rose so fast through the ranks. You were important. It was easy to convince them that we benefited from your being alive. It makes good sense, really.'

Nestor lashed out at Milton. 'So you kept me alive to milk me! Like... cattle! And I trusted you!'

Milton wiped a trickle of blood from his mouth.' Well, that was the reason I gave them.' He looked into Nestor's eyes. 'But no, the real reason was that I could never allow anyone to kill you, my friend.'

Nestor had turned away while Milton was talking. 'So that's why "not him"!' he whispered softly to himself.

'Exactly,' said Milton. 'They are fools, but they accept reason. I told them killing you would only make things more difficult.'

'Where do you meet to pass on the information?'

Milton said nothing.

Nestor turned away in rage. 'Bene, Solomon, all the others devoted to this country, what it should be one day. You betrayed all that! Never mind me, but for that betrayal you must die, or I must.'

Nestor scooped up the machete he had picked up on the way. He held it out hilt first to Milton.

Milton shook his head slowly, smiling to himself. 'Put it down. You know I am no match for you, and anyway there is something in me that would not allow me to harm you.'

'Take it!' Nestor roared. Then he stopped. 'But first, the meeting place. Where is it?'

Milton said nothing. He seemed to be thinking. Finally he rose to his feet and took the machete. 'Since you are determined that I am to die, it makes no difference.'

He gazed at the blade of the machete in his hand. 'Will you do something for me when I am gone? It will not

236

burden you too much.' Then he smiled mischievously. 'But first I must satisfy myself that you really will take my life!' He made a sudden lunge at Nestor with the machete and sliced through Nestor's shirt.

'You will now test *me*? Test *me*?!' roared Nestor, rushing forward.

As Milton had predicted, the contest was uneven. As Milton lay bleeding at Nestor's feet, his life slowly ebbing away, Nestor felt his rage being flooded out by the tears that welled up inside him. He sank to his knees beside Milton, whose eyes had turned glassy as he breathed blood in and out of his mouth. Milton gestured weakly to Nestor to come closer. Nestor moved over and cradled Milton's head in his arms.

'The grave... the meeting place... my wife's grave.'

Nestor took no notice. 'The request,' he said urgently. 'What do you want me to do?'

Milton seemed to regain a little strength. He grabbed Nestor's leg. 'Promise me... that you will take care of Titi. Shelter him from all this madness for me. Please. He is your child now.' Nestor nodded dumbly.

Long minutes he cradled Milton, watching him die, weeping quietly. When it was over, he let out a shattered cry.

In the village they sat glancing anxiously at each other in silence. When finally they heard the clash of metal and the sounds of battle they moved uncomfortably amongst each other. Then there was silence again. Long minutes later, a hideous cry rose and writhed away into the distance.

Kanu looked down at his feet, shaking his head. 'That is the fate of the vanquished,' he said.

# Twenty-nine

Philomena shivered silently. Nestor sat in the clearing outside, shoulders hunched, his eyes fixed upon the ground before him. He could be a rock, thought Philomena.

'Did you kill him?' asked Philomena.

'Yes,' he said. 'You saw.'

'Milton, I mean.'

Nestor was silent. Finally he said, 'You should go back to your home. You will never understand all this. And anyway, you did not come here because of your love for me. I am only one of the byways of your life. An important one, perhaps, but still no more. That moment when you said you would come with me, I knew you did not love me. Your voice said you were excited for something new, not happy that you would be with me. You came because it would always be a decision you could polish on your mantelpiece. You went to this savage place on an impulse. Your parents were horrified. You were so wild. You had kicked their codes in the teeth. Again. Even by your standards, this was the big one. Seven on the Richter scale. When you smiled and said you would go with me, you were smiling at the faces of your family when you told them. You were smiling at the new confusions it caused in their understanding of you. You were smiling at the prospect of new titillation to put bright new scratches on your jaded skin. Smiling at a million things, but not at Nestor Musambe. And it only made me want you more.

'Then we came here, and everything changed. Places change the balance between people. You were for the first time the innocent, the fair lady with the barrel of sympathy and no understanding.

Nestor came to her and took her roughly by the arm. 'Come.'

He led her out to the edge of the clearing. 'Look!' he said, pointing at a molten dusk. 'The dark continent you came to "experience"! What "dilemma"? What "question"? This is *us*. This is our life, what we *are*. The lion rules this land. Do you know why? Because he is the strongest. To be the strongest, he must kill. So he hunts down and kills cubs not to eat but only because if they grow up they become a threat to him. And he kills for food, to nourish his sinews. All his violences are acts of innocence. Simple, instinctive, devoid of malice. One day his sinews will give way to stronger ones, and he will be vanquished. And every day kingdoms are lost to the young and orders are changed. But the order remains the same. You want to know who we are? We are the lions. We are the cubs. We are life with all its terrors and beauties. You are the ones who want to rule the lions, who want to teach them to let the lioness help herself first at dinner before they dig in themselves. That is your arrogance.'

'So what happens inside men who butcher young boys?' asked Philomena archly.

Nestor shook his head and smiled. 'Everyone was once where we are now. They've moved on. Not forward or backward, just somewhere else. A new field, with different weeds and different harvests. Now they turn to us and presume to tell us what ails our fields and which one we must move to next. There is so much happiness here, happiness even in our sorrow, but the pain is all they can see. So they sandbag us with sacks of food and feel better. And we eat because our bellies are hungry, but another hunger is destroying us inside because there is a terrible sadness inside a man who must rely on the pity of others to eat.

'Our dying children and our convoys of dusty ghosts and our bleeding machetes and Milton and Titi and all the others are all little pieces of a very special dance. Today their blood, someday mine, will lend its special little splash of colour to it. And one day the dance will end in a great banquet and we shall feast on our *own* special food, food we have made *ourselves*.'

'I should have kept you in Bombay,' said Philomena, shaking her head sadly. 'I should have tried to keep the Nestor you were.'

'If I had stayed in India,' said Nestor. 'You would have disappeared from my life forever. I offered you your next adventure, and so you are here.'

Nestor sat down heavily on the ground. The sting of his last comment hung heavy in the air. Vacantly, he ran his hand over a smooth stone embedded in the ground, brushing away the dust that hid the tiny cracks on its surface. He looked up at Philomena, and if she had turned to look, she would have seen the softness and care of the Bombay Nestor in his eyes.

He rose and went to Philomena. Gently, he sat her down. When he spoke again, it was as if he had drifted away into his hidden life, the one that wrote poetry and told stories to the night.

'India,' he said slowly, 'was my holiday from life. Wonderful, bright with days of colour and innocence, with friendships that would die happy, on which no taxes were payable. I walked down troubled roads and the troubles would never be mine. I played with the happy dangers of Shapoor's debt collection and angry helicopter buyers. Monsoon nights standing alone on Chowpatty Beach feeling the rain sting my face. Afternoons spent in your arms, drinking tea from the chipped cup that your mother gave me every time.

'Then one day, I was sitting in the Pride, wondering what that bastard Kailash would cajole me into doing next. "West African …" said the discarded newspaper on the marble tabletop. I read the report. Two paragraphs on page thirteen. The military had almost completely overrun the troublesome east. Through this place, my home. What had happened? Pictures of the village being sacked raced through my mind. Our land. My village. Milton. Dad's hopeless dreams. What remained? What had been lost? Had anyone gained anything?

'"Oi Kaalu, What about yesterday's Bun Omelette payment?" Shapoor had trundled over to me. I looked

241

up, and he read the confusion in my eyes. His eyes glanced down at the newspaper, then back at me. He grunted and abruptly turned and shuffled back to his counter, shaking his head as he went.

'I sat there a long time. When I finally drank down the rose tea it was cold. I looked around, and saw Shapoor staring intently at me, scratching his grey stubble. The bugger's wondering how to make me pay my outstanding, I thought to myself. He's going to tell his cousin Minoo The Muscleman, who ferries racehorses from Bombay Central station to the racecourse on his shoulders for fun and rips out people's fingers if he needs a toothpick. I started to sidle out.

'"Oi Kaalu !" shouted Shapoor, crooking his finger at me. I went over. "Listen, you bleddy *chutia*, you are wasting your life. You are not to blame, I say. Everyone is doing it, because no one realises that this is not a dress rehearsal. One shot, bossy. The only one you will get. And at the end of the show, if you can't look up at the lights and smile, you might as well not have gone on the bleddy stage at all." He waved dismissively. "Now fuck off." As I turned away, he grabbed my arm. "Go home," he said, "Your main show is not here."

'Walking away, I heard him mutter, "And it will be cheaper for me."'

Philomena went over to the hut and brought out a lamp. The night was still. The flame held. Nestor lay down beside her and rested his head in her lap. His face flickered in the light.

'I walked every street in the city that evening,' he said. 'Packed as they were, they were deserted for me. I walked for hours and never saw a soul. I looked into doorways and only found darkness. I chased the squeaking of the bus brakes and saw the buses vanish in puffs of smoke. I saw a man I thought I knew and reached out to touch him. He just shrugged my hand off and walked away. He hadn't even looked at me, so how did he know he didn't know me? I sat in the worn trough of a marble step in the entrance to one of the great stone buildings at Ballard Pier, listening to the desolate whispers of a wandering wind.

'My gaze fell upon a stone on the pavement, and I don't know why, but I said softly: "And where are you from, old man?"

'The stone replied, "Have you seen the hills behind the lake at Powai? Well, I lived there. It was a good life, watching the village in the distance becoming a city. Sometimes in the winter people would clamber up and walk over me. They looked happy to be there, with the trees and the streams and us. Only the spiders troubled us, because they tickled. Then one day a different type of people came. Urgent, purposeful people. They threw cables around the place and left strange boxes behind. A little after they left, something happened. Even as I heard the explosion, we were flying through the air. We roared with pain as we fell and where we fell were the urgent people. They flung us onto a lorry and as we bounced away from the hills I looked back and saw livid gashes across my home. Then they dressed me (funny phrase, *dressed stone*) to look like all the other stones and laid me here."

'"Do you like it here?" I asked.

'"Ah, now that's a question," said the stone. "In the

beginning I hated it. The stuff they lay us in is all itchy, and my friends were all over the place, so I had to make new friends because the ones I really knew were all gone. New friends are never quite the same, are they? It was exciting, though. Horse-drawn carriages up to the Grand Hotel across there, and processions of fine people, and music from the ballroom. A civilised lot, the British. Two gentlemen in perfect evening dress even stopped once to examine me, and one of them said to the other "Damned fine stone on this pavement, eh?" Then they walked on, murmuring approvingly. Now it's just paunchy traders complaining about our unevenness. But I am resigned to being here now. It is my life now, and at the end of the day the life you live is the life you have. No point complaining if you do not do anything about it, and I know I can't. I would like to see my home on the hill again, but I have no choice, which makes things easy for me. Every day I remember a little bit less of it, and it remembers a little bit less of me."

'It just happened that walking home to the hostel I had to pass the Seaman's Club, with its huge noticeboard full of sailings and berthings and opportunities and offers. And there, in a sea of strange names and wondrous places was a tiny entry which said "Home" to me.'

'I should have kept you there,' repeated Philomena dully to herself. 'If home turned you from that person into this one, I should have kept you there.'

'I don't know, Phil... When you have houses and gardens and food and order assured to your life, your sights can turn to love and faith and what is "right" and what is "wrong". I will always love you...' He glanced quickly, almost shyly, at Philomena. 'You know that too. It is buried somewhere deep within me. And there it must stay, because these are things we cannot afford.'

Nestor fell silent, drawing invisible covers around himself with his arms.

'Yes,' he said.

'What?' said Philomena.

'Your question. Yes. I killed Milton.'

'Just like that?'

'He tried... to make it easier,' said Nestor. 'He looked straight at me and said, "Go ahead, my friend. One day perhaps we shall meet in a place where we are free to just be friends."'

Nestor turned abruptly and went towards the latrine. Shutting the bamboo door, he slumped down next to the pit. Furrows of hurt moved in formation on his forehead and he began to cry. The sobs whistled up from within, spilling misery and spittle over the latrine floor.

He cried for himself. Cried because he would never again see a sunbeam through a child's eyes. Cried for making the choices that made him kill the friend who had given his life for him and turn away the lover who he had fought for for so long. But most of all, he cried for all the times he should have cried but hadn't. Perhaps if he had wept in front of Philomena she would have understood a little more, but that did not happen – for him, the grief of men must remain behind locked doors in lonely rooms, and washbasins and walls are unforgiving companions.

When it was over and the emptiness complete, he wiped his face and made ready to face Philomena again.

Philomena looked up at him when he returned. 'I am leaving. There is nothing left for me to do here, no one left for me to do it for. I am so tired now, and you have more important fights to fight. Christopher has his new job, his new life... he doesn't even write any more. I will leave the day after you return from your council meeting – it will give me a few days to sort things out.'

Nestor nodded silently. Philomena went into the hut. A cold wind swept in from the savannah.

*

Nestor had walked this path home many times at each moment a day or night has to offer. Every turn, every ditch, every shadow was his home itself. But this night was strange, different, suffused with a silvery chill that took the breath away from the trees and left them stilled. A silent, torpid night, filled with promises of betrayal and the whisper of moonlit machetes.

The council meeting had gone badly. Nestor had sensed that had it not been for the Hook's restraining influence, the new members would gladly have damned him there and then.

He found his step quickening. The crickets sounded different tonight – confused, urgent. He lightened the crunch of his sandals on the gravel: this night demanded stealth. He knew he should sing for the snakes and the animals, but this night commanded the silence of true fear.

Old familiar shadows of rocks and trees along the path looked new, brooding. The shadow of the witch's claw of the baobab tree at the bottom of the hill lay across the path in a leprous fist tonight. Further along, the moon pushed through a bamboo thicket, and a shadowy net flowed over Nestor as he walked. Through the trees he caught an anxious glimpse of the distant lamplit hut and home.

Almost there now, he comforted himself. Round the right of the big round boulder in the middle of the path under Akimbo's Head, the lazy left-right sweep, and then the straight stretch up to the clearing before home. The muscles in his haunches tightened as his step quickened.

The shadow of the boulder was different. Fuller, unfamiliar on this mysterious night. As he rounded it, it moved and fragmented. Gliding swiftly on an invisible wind, it struck and struck again. Nestor fought and clawed and grabbed, but the hate and fury of those first few blows had already ended the duel.

This was not how it was supposed to have happened. It should have been a last sun-slashed charge at a hundred hated ideas. It could have been an execution, his eyes fixed on an African sunrise in his executioner's eyes. It should definitely have been by light, so he could watch his life drain its richness into the dust of this land he loved.

Yet here he was, dying quietly, struck down by petty hatred. On *his* path, which had conspired to change its face and rob him of even the comfort of dying at home, rob him of the death he had been born for and had lived for. One day this land will take my life... But *this*? A bitter smile dragged across his broken face.

Then the shadow struck again and the night poured its silence into him.

\*

Philomena switched off the transistor. It was a quarter to two. The wind was up again, and the mysterious stillness she had noticed earlier had been swept away. Tomorrow she would leave. She lay awake long, listening to the cries and exultations of her last glorious African night.

Nestor was not home yet. She listened through the noises and the wind for the crunch of his sandals. For the Nestor of the pink helicopters and the fluorescent windscreen. For the Nestor whom she had loved and spurned and loved again. For the Nestor who had loved her and loved her and left her for some higher love.

A chill wind slipped under her covers, billowing them gently in the moonlight. She dozed uneasily.

# *Thirty*

Philomena settled heavily into her seat on the plane. A stewardess came by offering palm wine to the passengers. Opening the plastic container she drank deeply. It was fresh and sweet. She read without interest the label on the container. '...Date of Expiry: 01.03.2003'. She gazed out of the window as the plane gathered speed and lifted off. Bathed in the early morning sunlight, the forest raced by beneath them, and as they gained height she turned to look into the distance beyond, to where the forest gave way to the scrub and the grasslands that had been her home for so long. Somewhere down there clothes fluttered brightly on a rusty gun turret. She had tried in her own way to help them vanquish the weapon they hung from, but the metal had endured and bitten back and defeated her.

As the plane turned its shoulder upon Africa, Philomena rummaged through her bag and pulled out the

letter Nestor had left her before leaving for his meeting.
She read:

'You are the only person I ever came close to showing
any of my poetry to. This is something I wrote about you
in Bombay a long time ago. If I have anything to regret
in my life, it is that we were never able to love each other
at the same time.'

Yours,

Nestor'

Philomena unfolded the poem.


### Untit.

There is no purity in the driven snow.
Don't question the statement – I should know.

I have ridden the mire, the grit and the straw,
A mercenary drifting with the luck of the draw.
And the rougher you get and the harder you grow,
The greater the fear of the dice's last throw.

You put your soul in the safe-box and your heart on hold,
And intensities, as ever, should be leaving you cold.

But you've used up all your callousness and cannot bear
    to think
Of the hollow, wasted emptiness from now to your next
    drink.

And the wheel stops
And the world turns
And the snow melts
And you
stop dancing.

Bombay, Jan. 1970

Philomena smiled a twisted smile. He could have been a poet, she thought to herself. He could have been a poet.

# *Thirty-one*

There were so many years for Philomena to sit and mull over, the many years before and since her return to Bombay. How she had pushed her way past the bewildered, traumatised tourists at the airport exit and found that the brutal chaos of this new India overwhelmed her too. How for days she had glared balefully at the crusty grey high-rise that obscured a chunk of the sea from the house. How she had sat and waited in vain for the longing for her son to deaden and drain away, and how Shirley Rajan had unexpectedly delivered up its secret to her one still summer afternoon.

\*

Chuckle.
Philomena stopped.
Chuckle, Chuckle.

It was a low throaty sound; rich, ancient and amused. Philomena instinctively knew that it was directed at her. Instinct apart, it could only have been directed at her – there was no one else there. Late afternoon was still siesta time in the village.

Philomena was strolling down towards the fish market along the road that ran by the sea. The morning fishermen were in and the afternoon fishermen were out. The fishermen's huts that lined the road slept in the heat. An occasional snore wafted out, and sometimes the clink of a vessel from an early riser. Even the public buses only came along every half-hour in the afternoon. The waves that usually crashed against the walls tiptoed in quietly.

The previous evening Arun Palitkar had jumped out of her past. The pimply poet was dead. Arun had moved to Singapore and become a successful architect with two grown children and a paraplegic wife to whom he seemed devoted. He had come by to see if the old house was still there and found Philomena sitting by the television. They had talked and talked and made slow, elderly love.

Now, walking along, Philomena was thinking to herself that it was strange that her first lover would probably also be her last.

'So, you took a man last night, eh?' said a voice.

Sameera. Moin's mother. Ninety-six, if a day, with a mind sharp as a razor.

Philomena turned and saw Sameera squatting on a *morah* in the deep shadows of the palm-frond awning that dipped low over the front of her hut. She smiled and walked over. Sameera was grinning mischievously, her single remaining tooth sitting snugly in the niche it had carved for itself in her lower lip. Her jaw moved steadily as she chewed tobacco. Philomena had always wondered how she managed to chew at all – perhaps she had a few malingering teeth inside.

Sameera motioned to Philomena to sit by her. Philomena let herself down slowly onto the step to the hut. She couldn't help liking this cheerful, leathery face with a huge tooth sticking out of it.

'How did you know?'

'What about?'

'Last night.'

'Ah, that's a long story,' said Sameera dismissively. 'You don't want to know.'

'I most definitely do,' said Philomena, determined to find out the extent of the intelligence network in the village.

Sameera did not appear to hear. Her eyes were hazy and distant when she spoke. 'It was a fine place, the Casa de Familia DaCruz, and your family was always the pride of the village: the DaCruzes, the Noronhas, and later the Fitters. And there were always the *safed* sahibs in the railway officer's quarters on Carter Road. Fine old fellows, and so polite. But you know, Ghanshyam the *dhobie* swore that they didn't bathe enough. He said that the smell on the bedsheets of the perfume and powder they poured over themselves never managed to hide the body odour.'

Philomena considered interrupting Sameera's afternoon ramble.

'Anyway,' said Sameera, 'as I was saying, your father was a good and fine man. How is he, by the way. Any news?'

Before Philomena could answer, Sameera continued: 'Your mother too, of course. In the beginning I would see them fooling about on the swing in the garden or walking together at the golf links or down to the jetty. They even came to the market once to buy fish from Moin. They were together then. When people are happy, there is a light that shines from within them that proclaims the beauty of the world. They had that light then. But they were married, and it's a funny thing, dearie, when people are married there is supposed to be some special *jaadoo*, and this magic is supposed to take care of everything forever. No money? No matter. No work? No matter. Nothing to say? No matter. Nothing left? So what – you're married!

'I watched the glow around them becoming smaller, till there were two separate glows, and much fainter, each going its own way – DaCruz *Saab* to the gymkhana, or that music of his, or work, or... I don't know. Where your mother was no one could tell.'

Holding on to Philomena's arm for support, Sameera leaned over and spat out the tobacco in her mouth.

'Yes, when that worm brother of yours was coming there was... something... again. But it was never going to make any difference. Poor Lancelot never had any spark in him to revive a glow. But still, they went everywhere as a family; to church to pray, to the golf links to play. In the car *sahib* would sit in his fine hat thinking of when he could expect to get away to the card room at the gymkhana, your mother would sit in her fine hat thinking of how unhappy she was, and Lancelot would sit in his big red bow tie thinking of... nothing.'

Sameera waved at a packet on the doorstep. Philomena handed it over. Opening it, Sameera dropped a tuft of tobacco into the palm of her hand and started kneading it with the thumb of the other.

'Then the pottery started. One day I saw a huge mound of clay by the wall near the *chikoo* tree – about there,' she said pointing to a spot in the distance. 'A potter's wheel arrived. Your mother would sit and mould for hours, without concern for food or drink or her child. In the day she worked to the sound of the cries of the street, and at night to the sounds of Edson *Saab*'s gramophone. In the burning sun and in the driving rain. But she did not make pretty pots or vases. The act of moulding seemed to be an end in itself. Her hands were only tools for the ache and emptiness coming from inside her. It flowed out through her hands, anointing the clay with a strange richness, pouring a special desolation into it. The sculptures themselves were beyond understanding – great big broken tears, twisted hearts with strange depressions and holes in them, pleading hands with melting fingers. Sometimes her fingers would fly over the clay in fury, but most often her hands caressed the clay, feeling, yearning, pouring out her emptiness into the clay.

'To most people, it looked like the clumsy work of any old novice. Maybe it was, but people started coming to see this possessed woman. Some even came in cars, and walked around your mother in a grave way, wisely pointing at some mysterious shape she had finished with, discussing clever things between themselves. What rubbish they talked! And using words even Edson *Saab* would not have understood! Analysing everything, understanding nothing. Tehmina *memsaab* would sit in the middle, moulding away as though they were not there. Sometimes some bold ones would try and speak to her, pointing at this sculpture or that. Who knows, maybe they wanted to know the price, I don't know. But I never saw her speak to even one. She would just look up at them and then turn back to her wheel. Day after day they would come, going round and round her, like the dancers in the glass dome clock in Fitter *Saab's* shop. A forest of clay figures grew around your mother, and this *tamasha* continued till…'

Sameera stopped, unsure of whether to continue. She looked around, as if seeking help. Seeing the determination in Philomena's eye, she set her lips and continued.

'It was a fair sky here, but in the distance a darkness was rising from the sea. I've never seen a sky so black with rain! Moin was standing where you are sitting now, wondering if he had enough time to bring his boat right up to the shore before the storm arrived.

'Just then your mother came out of the gate on one of her strolls up and down the jetty. She did not seem to notice the black horizon. "Madam!" Moin called out. "There is a storm coming." Your mother turned and looked at Moin. "So?" she said.

'Moin made as if to answer, then stopped. Their eyes locked, and my heart told me that something dangerous was happening. Moin turned and went into the hut. He returned with his leaky umbrella. Without a word he went over to your mother and fell into step. The first fat

257

drops fell on the roof of the hut. As they walked down the jetty, I watched as Moin opened the umbrella and offered it to your mother. She moved away. A little further, the scene was repeated – his offer, her refusal. They did not appear to talk at all till they reached the end of the jetty. Then words were exchanged, and this time your mother accepted the umbrella. But she didn't use it. She just dangled it around her knee, watching Moin pull in the tow rope of the little boat he used to paddle out to Naeema. The rain had become a torrent, and great sheets of water blew across my view. But I did see Tehmina *Memsaab* release the umbrella to the wind, and I did see Moin get into the little boat and hold his hand out to her, and when Moin started to undo the tow rope, I ran out towards the jetty.

'How my heart leapt and sank as I ran down the jetty fighting the wind and the rain. I thought of how I had tried to harness this primal son of mine. How a father might have helped. How for him, the paths he chose to walk had nothing to do with the others on them. How God had decreed that something was to happen between Moin and your mother that was not for human wisdom to understand or human effort to halt. At the end of the jetty, I stopped. I screamed. I shouted. I called out with all the desperation in my heart. But the wind was howling louder than me. They did not hear.

'They had reached Naeema now, and I sank to my knees and watched them struggle to board the pitching boat. The danger they were in suddenly came home to me. Only when they were on the heaving red hull did the tension flow away. And the fear rose again inside me.

'I flopped down on the cobbles. I pulled my knees up and dropped my head into them, too afraid of what I might see if I looked up. Around my ears the winds themselves seemed to tell me to leave, that I had not been invited here.

'It was true. I knew I did not belong in this moment. As I braced myself to make my way home, a scream rose across the waters and sliced a path clean through the wind and swirling rain. I looked up.

'Moin had pinned your mother's hips to the beam of the boat. The strength of his hold allowed her all the freedom she needed. And what freedom it was! Her hair, wet and heavy, whipped over backwards in whirling black arcs. Again and again. The fury of their lovemaking completed the wild canvas. They had merged with the thunder and the raging rain that hammered off their bodies and threw a sort of... misty sheath around them. How could I have ever hoped to hold reason up to these mighty forces?

'I walked away to the sounds of the crashing waves and the thunder and your mother's passion. I turned and looked sometimes, and each time turned away quickly again. The memory is like flashes, like photographs. All sorts of terrible, beautiful images. Of Moin's hand between her teeth. Of Moin's head between her legs, with her slumped over it...'

It had been Philomena's firm belief that she had long ago transcended the farthest frontiers of embarrassment, but she found herself squirming uncomfortably. Sameera's voice trailed off.

'Sorry,' said Sameera. 'I should have thought. Even

259

Moin only accepted that I could have had sex because his presence in this world forced him to!'

Philomena smiled and waved her hand. 'Go on,' she said softly.

'*Bus*, what's left? Oh, yes. The next day when I awoke the pottery, the wheel, everything, was gone. I never saw Moin and your mother alone again, but some weeks later I heard it again – your mother's cry, I mean. Late one night. Just once. But there was a difference. The cry was hers, no doubt, but it was different. Moin heard it too, because I looked over to his cot and saw his eyes shining white in the darkness, staring at the roof. We lay awake, waiting for another, but it never came and I realised what had been different. It was a moment of honesty in an act of deceit. That night I knew she was pregnant and had been since that afternoon with Moin. And last night I heard the cry again. Only this time it was yours.'

Sameera leaned back, her story done. They sat in silence for a while.

Then Sameera's brow furrowed. 'How she held out I don't know, but when you finally arrived it was many days past nine months since that afternoon with Moin. They said you were early, but I knew you were late. Moin knew too, but I could never bring myself to tell him of my knowledge. And when you were blind, I knew they had been punished. Moin knew too. I watched him suffer. Silently I watched my son's pain, pretending I knew nothing. The night you came back with your sight restored Moin disappeared.

'He had rowed out and sat alone on Naeema all night. When he came back at dawn he was drunk. And happy.

I have never seen him drunk *and* happy before. And I don't think it ever happened again. Maybe he was happy when he jumped off Santan's boat a few days after you left for Africa. But I don't think so. He was certainly drunk when Santan and he left, ranting away about swimming to Portugal! Santan said he had announced to him that he was jumping off Santan's boat and not Naeema so it wouldn't be seized and I could get a little money from selling her.'

Sameera got up and stared out at the bay. 'Fool!' she said in a low voice. 'As if it was Naeema I needed!'

She turned and shuffled back to the *morah*, letting herself down with a sigh. 'I was so angry. In my rage I decided to reject his bequest. I went out to Naeema on an ebbing tide and cut away her moorings. On my way back I did not once turn to watch her drifting away, because I had decided that I would not allow myself any sorrow. When I reached here I half-looked, expecting to see a black mast in the distance. But there she was, exactly where she is now – jammed on the rocks, refusing to break up, refusing to die, though she will never sail again. What to do?' Sameera threw up her hands in resignation, as though closing the discussion.

Philomena stared intently at Sameera. Her grandmother. Weather-beaten, unbroken. In the old days she would have thrilled at the fact that she was a fisherman's illicit daughter. Now she only felt a gentle confusion and a little happiness at finding a piece of real family.

'Will there be any *rawas* left in the market?' asked Philomena. It was almost seven o'clock.

'Go and see.'

On the way back from the market she bought a bottle of *santra* – cheap, harsh, and 'Government-Approved' – and gently hectored Sameera into accompanying her home.

As they mounted the steps to the veranda, Sameera asked again: 'So how is Edson *Saab*? Still working with his cousin?'

Saying nothing, Philomena shuffled over to the mantelpiece. Setting down the bottle of liquor, she read from a small newspaper cutting: 'The Hong Kong police recovered the body of an elderly man of Indian origin from the sea near the Kowloon Star Ferry terminal late last night. The body was identified by relatives as that of one Mr Edson Victor DaCruz. No injuries were found on the body. A mysterious degeneration of the skin on the little finger of the right hand was noticed, which sources stated was consistent with symptoms associated with prolonged immersion in alcohol. The authorities stated that no foul play was suspected.'

Sameera looked away.

After a while, she asked in a puzzled voice, 'Why would he dip a finger in alcohol?'

'To stir his rum. Always did.'

Sameera was quiet. 'A lot of rum, then,' she murmured.

Philomena put the piece of paper down carefully, and opened the bottle of *santra*. Wincing at the smell, she carried it out to the veranda and she sat down on one of the crumbling cane chairs on the veranda, motioning Sameera to sit too. Sameera looked around hesitantly, then sat down on the floor at Philomena's feet. Philomena stared down at her grandmother on the floor.

'Fine, I'm fine,' muttered Sameera, pre-empting Philomena's protest. Philomena continued to gaze down at Sameera. Suddenly she was overcome by the desire to laugh. Her mouth twitched and she giggled. Still giggling, she got up and let herself down onto the floor beside Sameera, who began to chuckle at the sound of Philomena's bones creaking their protest.

They laughed a lot that night, by the light of the bare bulb that hung in the veranda. About things and people gone away: little Fali Fitter caught vigorously masturbating behind the counter of his father's shop; Mackie, the mad baker, enthusiastically digging his nose in his shop and announcing, '*Chee*, men, how much dirty my nose is inside! Being clean is most important in my line.' Little quirks and anecdotes which only insiders knew or found amusing. For a few drunken hours, amidst the peeling paint and the crickets in the dark, tangled garden they ferreted out ghosts from the past, snatched back pieces of a village lost and gone.

# *Thirty-two*

Philomena had asked Carla to write and tell her of Christopher, and this Carla had done faithfully. But a few days after Sameera had told Philomena the secret of her parentage, Carla wrote to say that Christopher was rapidly rising through the ranks of the new government. Soon after, she wrote again that she would prefer to not write about his movements any more even if she knew about them, which more often than not now she didn't. Carla never wrote to Philomena again, and Philomena suspected that she had always deep down somewhere seen Philomena's leaving as an act of abandonment.

Some months later Philomena was sitting on the veranda watching the sun set over the terrace of the building in front of the house that so offended her when a black limousine pulled into the driveway and stopped. An African gentleman in a dark suit got out and strode up to Philomena. He stood before her and snapped his heels smartly.

'Miss DaCruz?'

Philomena nodded.

The man held out an envelope. Philomena took it, and her heart jumped. The handwriting on the cover was Christopher's – perhaps he was coming to see her! She looked up with excitement at the man, but he smiled and held up his hand. Bowing crisply, he turned and left.

Philomena opened the envelope with trembling hands.

'Mother,

I do not know whether it will please you or not to know that after a painstaking search by my personnel amongst the carnage around the village, we have succeeded in discovering the remains of my father, Nestor Musambe, which have now been laid to rest with the full state honours that befit a hero of the revolution.

Clutched in the skeleton of his right hand was the necklace you never ever took off – the one with the pendant in the shape of a boat. You will observe that the chain is snapped, as if violently snatched from the neck of the wearer.

I have tried very hard not to question the propriety of your killing him or speculate about your reasons for doing so. I hold, as you presumably know, a position of great importance and responsibility in this country, a natural consequence of which is that I also have many powerful enemies. It would be catastrophic for me to be discovered to be the son of my father's killer, of Nestor Musambe's killer – God knows I have had to struggle hard enough to overcome the illegitimacy of my origin that you and Father so casually bestowed upon me. Our correspondence is therefore necessarily at an end. You may at least follow my fortunes through the newspapers or television. I am not so fortunate.

I do still brush my teeth after lunch, and my hair is now cropped close enough to not show that I do not brush it often!

> I will always remain
> your loving son,
> Christopher Musambe

PS I urge you most fervently, for my sake, to destroy this letter.'

Philomena stared at the letter, clutching the pendant in her hand. Slowly, reluctantly, she began to tear it up the letter. Halfway down the page she stopped. Folding it up, she slipped it back into its envelope.

She looked down at the pendant, at the *dhow* that her fisherman father had given her mother and that her mother had given her after imploring her to never tell her other father about it.

She rose and shuffled across to the mantelpiece and placed the envelope carefully behind Nestor's poem. The pendant and chain she laid down gently on the faded velvet inside the box with the Queen's photograph on it.

Staring vacantly at the television later that night, a face suddenly flashed before her eyes. A dashing young West African foreign minister was delivering a major speech at the United Nations in New York on the 'patronising of Africa by the West'. Philomena feasted her eyes upon Christopher as she snapped from channel to channel, frantically chasing the images of her son. She sat up the whole night and half the next day, till the clip finally dropped out of the news altogether. Then she slowly got to her feet, pulled out an old writing pad from Edson's bureau and wrote down a date on it for the first time: '26.1.2008'.

From that day, she watched the news channels incessantly. Now, so many years on, there were three, maybe four more dates neatly written below that first entry. Quite a lot of coverage for a young minister from a small country in Africa, not much for a broken mother.

*

When her brother called to say he was planning a visit to Bombay, Philomena was bemused. Lancelot had never returned from England, not once. Perhaps he wanted to convince her to sell the house, perhaps he had decided that his soul longed for a quick, time-bound trip to his 'roots' – Philomena was past caring. Please God, let him bring the rain with him, she thought to herself. The rain was late, so late this year...

Lancelot did not tell her when he would be arriving, so Philomena looked up anxiously when a blanched little man in an exhausted jacket and tie alighted from a taxi and ascended the steps late one night.

Philomena stared at him. He put down a blue bag with the words 'Curtis Travels' across it and walked over to her.

He embraced her stiffly. 'Phil,' he said.

'Lancelot,' she said.

She showed him to an unmade room and handed him some sheets and a towel. Then she went back to the hall and quickly cleared away her things from the mantelpiece.

After a while, when he did not emerge from the room, Philomena went over and found her brother asleep on the unmade bed. He was smiling happily to himself in his sleep. She switched off the light and shut the door gently behind her.

The next day, they talked of this and that, from time to time lapsing into the kind of silence in which each one furiously tries to find things to revive the conversation with. Philomena could see that Lancelot had something on his mind, and that he was apprehensive about broaching the topic.

As they sat silently sipping their tea that afternoon, Lancelot finally spoke. 'Phil,' he said. 'I worked hard for thirty-two years. Ten thousand mornings I have woken up in the same room. Ten thousand tube rides to St Paul's, ten thousand more to get home again. Nine to six for ten thousand days. My desk has changed four times, each time getting a little larger. I even had a cabin to myself at the end. They have been good to me, because I have been good to them. Irene is a good wife and a good mother, and I've tried to be a good husband and father. On Sundays we always go to the pictures, and sometimes to Richmond Park when it's not to cold and the sun is out. For thirteen years I took Kevin to every home game Tottenham played, except once when he had the mumps and thrice when my back played up. And I have been a good husband too.'

Lancelot leaned forward conspiratorially. He hesitated a moment and then continued. 'Well I may as well tell you, seeing as you are hardly likely to be bothered. I've had an *affair*!' he said, his voice dropping to a triumphant whisper. 'Many years ago, and only a week or so it lasted. Nice she was too, and exciting, but Irene is a good girl and I couldn't break our hearts for... for *that*. So I ended it. It wasn't easy, but it had to be done,' he said proudly.

Philomena smiled, and if Lancelot had been the kind of person who noticed such things, he would have seen from the softness in her eyes that she too was in her own strange way proud of him. She leaned back and closed her eyes, picturing Lancelot sitting cosily in his suburban haven every evening watching tomorrow's weather forecast on the television through his double-glazed spectacles, while she had been reaping whirlwinds. A trickle of regret ran through her.

'Anyway,' started Lancelot again. 'That is not what I came here for. Thing is, Irene is a big-hearted girl, and we have been discussing this a lot. You see, Kevin doesn't live at home now, so his room is empty. We thought it proper to ask him first anyway, and he has agreed.'

Lancelot leaned over and placed a hand over Philomena's. When he spoke his voice was urgent with affection. 'Come and stay with us in England. I am all you have left,' he said. 'Me and this house and the memories. You have searched and stalked and found and always it was not what you had been stalking. It is time to try a different tack. A hard way, and harder for someone like you. You are too stubborn to believe it, but I *am* happy. I am happy because I have not searched for the promised land, because if it could be found it wouldn't be promised any more. Come with me.'

A wry, soft smile crept up from Philomena's lips into her eyes as she gazed out over the bay. England! The spiritual home of the DaCruzes! Handel and Elgar. Misty downs and Rupert Brooke, the Rolling Stones and Bush House and Brighton Rock. Ah, she'd missed this one! But then it was always so.... *obvious*. Come to England, she thought. New people to deal with, new windmills to tilt at, new attitudes to break, new people to conquer. It was all too much, too late. It was over. She had raged her storms, walked her gangplanks. Paid her taxes, no rebates. Her ship was in, bobbing peacefully on calm waters. There it was, sitting in the bay, black mast and red hull.

She had been born blind, like everyone else, and had fought to see. And she had learned to see like so few others, learned the hard way that the trick to life was not to experience everything, but to learn in the attempt to rest happy with knowing that searches do not end with treasure chests, only resolution.

'No,' she said to Lancelot, who already knew. Watching her eyes, for the first time he had seen the spirits that danced in them fade and take the life from her.

The first fat drops of rain fell upon the thirsty bramble outside.

*

How many times after that day did Philomena sleep and awaken and eat and wash? How many more monsoons did she see, and how many were late and which ones arrived early? Did Lancelot ever visit her again? Did Christopher never make the long journey to the Casa de Familia DaCruz to hold his father's killer in his arms? It does not matter. Life ends when a person abandons the living of it. The body often lingers, like an old red hull listing gently on stilled waters.

# Acknowledgements

Many thanks to Rebecca Gould for helping open the perfect door, Kathryn Gray and Richard Davies in the room within at Parthian for believing in the book and for all the hard work to bring it to the place it's at, and Arshia Sattar for her unstinting generosity and invaluable advice.

To Pheroze for all the help over the years, and most of all to Anu, for her unwavering support of the dream through the many times it seemed to make much more sense to just wake up.

# PARTHIAN

## Contemporary International Fiction

## Writing in Translation